Murder on Her Mind

by

Glenys O'Connell

Dedication

I owe a huge thank you to my very patient husband, Adrian, and the friends who never doubted me even when I was engrossed in planning murders.

Prologue

Night-time village streets magnify and distort sounds.

Running footsteps sound like rapid heartbeats.

Screams are like the call of foxes in the undergrowth.

Cries for help go unheard.

No one answered Ralph's pleas as he cowered in the dark alley between the feed store and the bait shop, where he'd tried to hide from his pursuers. The first person stepped forward into a shaft of moonlight and, recognizing, Ralph laughed. His laughter was partly at himself for being so afraid and partly at them because they were such harmless jerks. What could they do to him?

But he was angry, too, at this affront to his dignity.

"It's you..." He growled, pulling himself up, "Having a joke, were you? You'll pay for this, you stupid..."

He stopped laughing as the first knife blade sank deep into his gut. He screamed as the knife rose and fell, a name spoken softly at each raising of the blade. He stopped screaming when the last thrust penetrated his heart.

Ralph Morris died with comprehension slowly dawning in his eyes.

Chapter One

Old Harry Jakes staggered out of his falling-down house onto his back porch, clutching an open beer bottle in one hand and a lit cigarette in the other. His grizzled face screwed up in a squint as the sharp afternoon sunlight hit his swollen, alcohol-reddened eyes.

Next door, the Logan family, damned yuppie scum, were enjoying a Thanksgiving Day barbecue, and the sound of laughter drifted across the scruffy patch of grass between the two houses.

Harry hated the Logans. He hated the way Pete Logan and his two teenaged sons joshed each other, laughed together, worked together, occasionally fought and always made up. He hated the way Pete and his pretty wife Angela sat quietly on their porch in the evening, content with their upwardly mobile lives. He hated the way the sounds of their lovemaking drifted through the open windows on summertime evenings and filled him with a longing for something—he didn't know quite what, but something he'd never known. Family, perhaps, or love. Or maybe just regular sex. Whatever, Harry hated the Logans. Sometimes he fell asleep, a few beers under his belt, and awoke from wet dreams of giving Angela Logan the good poking he figured her husband was too much of a wimp to satisfy her with. He hated them for that, too.

He hated them even more now, after Todd Leech

had visited. The building inspector told him his house was a disgrace to the village and not fit for human habitation. Not fit indeed—hadn't Harry lived there for years, and no one gave a toss what a man did on his own property? Harry figured someone must have complained about the state of the place. Granted, it was a bit untidy, what with the ongoing yard sale through the summer and the bits and pieces of old cars and machinery he tinkered with, but damn it all, a man had a right to make a living.

Harry guessed someone had been tattling to the municipal council and that was what had sparked that lazy bastard Leech—well named, eh?—to drag his butt all the way out to Jacques Station and threaten to condemn Harry's home if he didn't fix the place up. Thirty days he'd given him, when the house had taken thirty years to get into this state! Now Harry figured that one of the newcomers to the village, the ones snapping up the cheap houses and tarting them up with new paint and extensions, sunrooms, and solar lights, had complained that his place was keeping property values down.

And the likeliest of them all was Pete Logan. Harry was willing to bet the nice little cash stash under his mattress that Logan had set Leech on him. Anger stirred him, rippling through his alcohol-pickled brain and flaring into blazing life. He scowled blackly as one of the Logan sons, Pete Junior probably, made some snarky remark to his dad and was rewarded with a deep belly laugh. *His* dad had never tolerated something like that! No, his old man would have gotten out his grandma's walking stick from behind the back door and pelted his hide till he begged for mercy and promised never to be disrespectful again.

Harry's gaze lingered on the pile of garbage near his back porch steps. Damned council had put the dumping charges up. How was he going to get his yard cleaned up if he couldn't afford to get rid of the waste? He'd go bankrupt taking all this stuff down to Overmere to the dump. He eyed up the pile of branches from the tree that had come down in last winter's windstorm, and the two old settees that were quietly rotting into the ground. They'd be damp, but they'd still burn....

Harry put his beer down and went across the yard to drag the furniture over to the garbage pile, adding the branches till the pile was almost as high as his roof.

He rooted around in his garden shed till he came up with a gas can that was half full of fuel for the lawn tractor that hadn't started in a year or so and added its contents to the pile. Then he threw a lighted match on the whole thing and, picking up his beer, went back onto his porch, sat on the sagging recliner by the back door, and watched the fire flicker, die down, then take hold with a resounding whoosh as flames reached for the sky...and smoke rolled and billowed from the damp upholstery and plastic.

Harry grinned as he heard the shouts from next door, the sound of scurrying feet as the Logans' barbecue was enveloped in acrid black smoke. Why, he even thought he heard Mr. Family Man Logan shout a curse word or two before the windows of the house were slammed shut.

Yes, sirree, if the Logans wanted Harry to tidy up his yard, well, that's what he was doing, wasn't it?

Harry finished his beer contentedly listening to the snap and crackle of the fire. The old man fell asleep, but the fire didn't. Some minutes later Harry wakened briefly to scream as the fire enveloped him and his little house as an appetizer to what came next.

****

Being an equal opportunity destroyer, the fire leaped and zigzagged around the village, riding the coattails of a summer breeze to light here on this house, skip over that house, land again on the abandoned Anglican church but leave the recreation hall untouched....

The roar of fire and the choking smoke brought neighbors out from across the village, trying to understand the emergency as the small volunteer fire department raced through the streets. There were shouts of horror as villagers began to grasp the reality of the monster that was destroying their homes even as they watched.

Already Jim MacDonald, the fire chief, realized the blaze was too big to handle and called for help from brigades all across the county. Soon the night sky along Highway 7 was lit with blue and red lights as fire, police, and ambulance emergency vehicles raced towards Jacques Station, a tiny Ontario village that hardly anyone had heard of but which would be thrust into its fifteen minutes of fame on that evening's television news.

****

Spirals of smoke still drifted through the village streets like the ghosts of revelers unable to find their way home as dawn came the next morning. Like most of the other people in Jacques Station—the able-bodied ones, anyway—I had been up all night on fire watch. My hands were skinned raw from working with my neighbors to form human bucket chains from the mill pond to tamp down the smaller fires that lit on grass and park benches, garden gazebos and arbors, even parked cars that their owners hadn't been able to move in time. The collective thinking was simple: if we could keep the small fires down, the multiple fire departments could handle the big blazes and concentrate on saving our homes.

The reality was that, faced with catastrophic loss, even neighbors who didn't particularly like each other saw the need to pull together, and to cling to each other's company for safety. Doing something, anything, was better than watching our village devoured by fire, and action kept the darkness away.

Now, as dawn was breaking, the full extent of the damage could be seen. Exhausted, I sat on the concrete stoop of my big century home, heartbroken and shocked at what was slowly being revealed as the sun rose over Jacques Station.

I rubbed my throat, aching and raw from inhaling smoke, and shook my wheat-colored hair loose from the unruly ponytail I'd clipped it in during the night, idly wondering if the trauma would add another streak of grey. They say shock does that.

My tired mind could not shake off the creeping melancholy as I stared down the main village street where only the day before elegant homes and tiny bungalows, scruffy lots and well-kept modern houses had lain together sleepily quiet in the autumn sunlight.

Now at the far end of Queen Street on the bend before the untouched public school, Harry's house was nothing more than smoking ashes. The Logans' home next door was reduced to a blackened ruin. Then the fire had skipped over the general store and, thank God, the gas station, to sate itself on the lumberyard and feed store. The general store's new summer-smart paintwork sported streaks of black soot and ugly blisters where the paint had bubbled in the heat from the roof of Abe

Smith's cottage next door. The cottage roof was burned into holes from which wisps of grey smoke still rose. Abe himself was sitting on the pavement across the street, staring with empty eyes at the home his grandfather had built when Jacques Station was a thriving logging community. I had to look away because I couldn't bear the sight of the old man wiping tears from his eyes.

Farther down the street the little craft store and coffee house owned by Tony Bonvieux and Will Clements, Jacques Station's celebrated gay couple, was blackened but intact, and the town library was spared.

Around the corner, the township offices had barely been touched but smoke still rose from the ruined stonework of the Anglican Church, closed and unused this past ten years. The church's stained-glass windows had survived years of neglect, bitter cold winters, and scorching summers, and had never yet felt the wrath of stone-throwing vandals. Now the colored glass littered the ground and I wished with all my heart that I'd actually got around to photographing the windows in all their glory. Now it was too late.

"We always think we have so much time," I whispered to nobody in particular.

"It's burned down twice before, you know." I startled at the rich deep voice behind me. I had not heard Alex McGeary approach, I was so deep in my own thoughts and grief. The village reeve needed no invitation to sit down wearily next to me on the cold cement stoop. We were old friends from childhood when the kids here in Jacques Station had roamed wild and free. "Once in the 1870s, and again in the 1900s. Both times it was all lightning strikes and fireballs from the sky."

"Do they know where it started this time?" I gratefully accepted the cup of coffee Alex offered me. Ron and Sue James, owners of the Last Drop Bistro, had opened up during the night and joined with Will Clements and Tony Bonvieux from Crafts and Coffee to hand out a constant supply of coffee and sandwiches to weary villagers, firemen and emergency crews as the hours wore on.

"I talked to the fire chief and unofficially they're thinking the fire started in a pile of rubbish outside Harry's back porch. How it caught fire is another matter and—well, they've found Harry. What's left of the poor old sod."

As head of the village council, Alex is privy to all sorts of information ordinary mortals couldn't access. "I wish…I wish we'd made the old reprobate clean up his lot earlier. Maybe we could have avoided all this. Or maybe we shouldn't have harassed him at all." Alex ran a weary hand over his eyes. He'd lived here all his life, and his father before him had been reeve, probably his granddaddy as well.

I swallowed coffee around the lump that had formed in my throat and reached out to pat his arm. There was little comfort I could offer to a man who felt his responsibilities to our little community so deeply and would always mourn the losses the village had sustained this night.

He'd even mourn old Harry. *Probably we all will.* Despite his bad behavior, Harry Jakes had been a character who'd tied Jacques Station back to its earlier, tougher days before the wealthy outsiders had discovered the Land O' Lakes and moved in to upgrade the cheap properties into elegant summer homes by the lakes of Eastern Ontario. Since that had happened the village has been in danger of losing its identity, its soul.

Old curmudgeons like Harry reminded us all of where we came from. We'll all mourn him once the pain eases a little.

"It's not your fault, Alex. Harry lived his own life. He was probably drunk and in charge of a lighted cigarette or something." I patted Alex's arm again and wished I had more words of comfort for him and for the rest of the shocked and devastated folk wandering around the streets.

For the first time in my life, I understood the bitter resentment aimed at the television and newspaper reporters who seemed to be turning our loss and sorrow into a sensational sound byte for people who had never been here, would never know what this was like, and would forget us as soon as the next tragedy occurred.

"I'd like to punch one of them," I told Alex, pointing to a news crew who roamed the street, and he grinned.

"You're not alone in that one, Gracie, but just imagine—Jacques Station is going to be known throughout Ontario. People throughout the province—maybe even the country—will be talking about us at breakfast!"

"Yeah, and like they'd care. Jacques Station will be forgotten before nightfall when some new shiny bauble of disaster comes along."

"Maxie, Maxie! Where are you, kitty? Come on home!" The wavery voice of Mildred Cairns cut into our conversation. *Lord, but Millie loved that old cat, Maxie.*

"What's the matter, Mrs. Cairns? Are you all right?" I called to the old woman in her pajamas and bunny slippers, her thin iron-grey hair sticking out at odd angles as she wandered by. She had a lost and confused look that tugged at my heartstrings.

"Oh, it's you, Gracie," she replied. At least she recognized me. That didn't always happen these days, although we were close neighbors.

"Did you lose your glasses?" I said, slipping my arm around her fragile shoulders.

"What, dear? My glasses…" She reached a brown-spotted hand to her face, surprised they weren't in their usual perch on her wide nose. "Oh, yes, I guess I must have. There was a fire, you know…."

"I know." I turned her to look at me, trying to pull her back into reality. Everyone knew Millie was slowly slipping into senile dementia. "Are you looking for Maxie?"

Tears rolled down her wrinkled face, falling onto her flannel pj top as she nodded. Alex offered her a napkin from around his coffee cup and she wiped her eyes. "Maxie was frightened of the fire and all the alarms and sirens, and he tore open the window screen and ran out before I could grab him. Now I don't know where he is."

Losing that cat would be enough to kill Millie, who was eighty-nine if she was a day and had no other family. "Come on, Mrs. Cairns. We'll go look together for Maxie. Two pairs of eyes are better than one." I looked over at Alex, who slumped wearily still on my door stoop. He nodded at me, and I walked along the street towards the burned-out hulk of the feed store, Millie leaning heavily on my arm.

"Maxie likes to come in here—there are always lots of mice to catch…rats, too, I'd say. With all that grain and animal feed, you know." Millie kept up a running conversation in between calling her cat's name.

Looking at the blackened rafters that were all that remained of the feed store, I offered a little prayer to the patron saint of felines that Maxie had not taken refuge there. The moth-eaten old tomcat would be toast if he had. Along, probably, with all the rats and mice that ate into the feed store's profits, according to Malcolm Etherbridge, who owned the place.

Malcolm was standing in the middle of the road, gazing at his ruined business, his ball cap pushed back over his head, his normally perky handlebar moustache drooping like the rest of him. His face was blackened with soot stain, but there were tear tracks down his cheeks.

"It's all gone, Gracie. Everything I worked for is ashes now. Did you know that my Grandaddy Etherbridge, the one who came here from Scotland, founded this business? And now, in a single night, it is all gone. What am I going to do now?"

"I don't know, Malcolm. I don't know. I guess we'll all have to help each other cope." Words, words. They slip so easily from our lips and carry as much weight as dandelion seeds in the wind.

A pretty young woman in a pink power suit clattered up to us, her high heels precarious on the rough road that there was never enough municipal money to grade and surface. "We're with the television news and we'd like to interview you about this terrible tragedy," she purred, her microphone pushed out towards Malcolm and her eyes predatory.

Malcolm must have looked like a prize to her, the quintessential old fart that her like expected to find in these backwoods villages. I braced myself for the

11

response, which wasn't long in coming.

"Why don't you and your like piss off and leave us to get on with our lives? Can't you see there's work to be done here? And you know where you can shove your condolences—and you can shove the mike up there as well!"

Malcolm glared her down and the woman, her cheeks flaming red, backed off and scurried away, no doubt muttering to her camera man about the low-life Neanderthals who lurked in these forgotten places.

Suddenly Millie shook off my hand and took off towards the still smoldering beams of the feed store, calling out, "Maxie! Maxie! You're all right! Come to Mommy!"

I took off after her, terrified that she would fall and be killed in the still smoking ruins, or that the one tottering wall that leaned out over what used to be an alleyway would topple on her.

Millie reached the cat, who was cowering in a corner against the stone foundation. She scooped him up into her arms, muttering calming words as if to a child. She stood a moment smothering his flea-bitten coat with kisses as I reached her and grabbed her arm to support her ahead of me and out of harm's way.

Following her, I stumbled over something and had to grab the still hot stones to save myself from falling headlong. When I looked down and saw what I had tripped on, bile rose in my throat.

It took me a horrified moment to find my voice and shout to Malcolm, who was helping Millie back out onto the road, to call the police.

"Get them right now!" I yelled at him as he started to come into the alleyway to see what was causing me such concern.

His eyes widened. "Jesus Christ! I'll get the paramedics…."

"No, Malcolm. Just get the police. I think this poor soul is well past the need for medical help."

****

My name is Gracie Pelham, and I live in the house my great-grandparents built in this village of Jacques Station. Much of my childhood summers were spent here, until I went out into the wide world, intent on saving those in need, as a psychologist.

But Jacques Station always called me back. I married a police detective, Ben, and we had a pretty daughter together. But our little Becky disappeared and has never been found, and our marriage couldn't take the strain.

Ben and I still meet occasionally. He cannot refrain from criticizing me for trying to save the world, and I cannot agree with his uncharitable view of lawbreakers, so we tend to circle each other and growl like two angry cats. I received divorce papers from him, signed them, and sent them back to him for his signature. He hasn't signed yet and claims he is just too busy.

Chapter Two

As the first days after the devastating fire passed, lack of sleep and a small dose of Post-Traumatic Stress Syndrome began to take its toll on the residents of Jacques Station. In the echoing space of the United Church Hall, I saw my own numbness and sense of unreality reflected in the expressions of the villagers huddled there. It was stark on the faces of the volunteers doling out coffee and sandwiches and whatever comfort they could, in the movements of the men and women who walked around aimlessly or sat staring into space, and on the slumped and exhausted shoulders of our volunteer firefighters.

Our friends and neighbors had fought the demon fire and, despite their valiant efforts, had lost so much. Suddenly the emptiness of all my years of training as a psychologist, and all the endless hours of counselling I'd taken and given, weighed on my shoulders. These people were friends and neighbors, people I'd known most of my life, yet nothing in all my education and training offered a way to show them a kernel of comfort. All the little tricks of the therapy trade, the silent pauses, the incisive questions, the reflecting of a client's feelings, none of these were working now. I had nothing in my therapist's bag of tricks that could help anyone recover from this ordeal, least of all myself.

"Oh, Gracie—I'm so sorry! To have worked like a

dog to fight the fire, and then to find…to find…was it really horrible?" Allice Spence, Allie to her friends, church minister and all-round extraordinary woman, slipped into the seat beside me and wrapped her arms around me in a much-needed hug.

"About as bad as it could get." The horror of that barbecued body, the burned skin splitting and the terrible, stretched grimace of the face, came back to mind and I couldn't shut it out.

Allie grabbed my hand and pulled me to my feet. "Come back to my office—I've a little something in a bottle that'll help. Purely medicinal," she added loudly for the benefit of Miss Jodie and her brother, Mr. Peter, who'd turned shocked teetotaler faces towards their minister as they overheard her words. Miss Jodie sniffed and looked away, but Mr. Peter gave us a quick wink before looking back down at the magazine he was reading.

****

The warmth of the brandy Allie produced from her desk drawer went some distance towards lifting the chill that had seeped into my soul ever since I had seen that poor burned boy.

"Did…were you able to tell who it was?" Allie was trying to be delicate, but there was no way not to tread like an elephant around the subject.

"No, I think it was a boy, maybe a young man, but it was…well, there wasn't too much left of the face."

"Do you think he was a local boy? We've not come across anyone unaccounted for yet, but some of the kids from the townships were in the village earlier for a baseball game."

I shrugged. I didn't know who the poor soul was; I

just wished his image would leave my head. "I'm not sure I'll sleep again without seeing him, not for a long time. So, my friend, where was God in all this?"

My professional diagnosis of my behavior was shock, but somehow I could not stop myself attacking my closest friend's deeply held beliefs. "So again, my friend, where was God in all this?" I repeated.

"You have no idea how many times I've been asked that question. But that is why we call it faith—we believe there is some higher reason behind the things we consider to be disasters."

"So somehow God has got a plan that will bring Jacques Station through this 'tragedy' into a better world?"

"Well, they do say an event that to the caterpillar is the end of the world is also the beginning of something beautiful for the butterfly."

"You are kidding, right?"

"I know you don't believe, but…"

"What I don't believe is that anyone would consider that Jacques Station could morph into something beautiful like a butterfly."

And just like that we were both laughing, our bodies shaking with mirth so hard that we wound up clutching each other for support.

The laughter was short lived, for at that moment our peace was shattered as the office door was thrown open and Tina Hayes, probably my least favorite person on the planet—after my ex-husband—stormed in.

"Oh, now isn't this cozy? You just never miss a chance to get up close with Allie, do you, Doctor Pelham?" Tina sneered, perching her skinny ass on the edge of Allie's chair and grabbing hold of her hand, effectively barricading my best friend from me.

We sat in silence for a little while. Allie's face was serene, and I knew she was praying to the God she devoutly believed in. An underpinning of our friendship was that she never tried to make me a convert to a mystery I could not accept. But then, in my line of work, I think I've seen too much of the evil and not enough of the divine in people.

"Tina, we were just talking…Gracie's had an awful shock…" Allie finally spoke, but Tina overrode her.

"I heard about her crispy-critter find. Bet she's milking it for all it's worth. Did she get you to offer comfort and affection?"

"Aw, shit, Tina, stuff it where the sun doesn't shine," I growled, slamming my glass down on the desk and stalking from the room. I couldn't stand Tina, her possessiveness, her jealousy, her constant state of anger and chip-on-the-shoulder routines.

As if I could give a rat's ass that she was lesbian. As if I could give a rat's ass that my best friend had "come out" barely a year ago and had the bad taste to get involved with the loathsome Tina.

What I hated was the constant attempt to drive a wedge between the two of us, to sideline our friendship.

The Lord that Allie preached about had to know I needed a friend right then.

But He obviously wasn't paying attention, because as I walked out of the church hall, I was hailed by the one person I really did not want to see.

I especially did not want him to see me like this, after a sleepless night, exhausted rings around my eyes, smoke and grime everywhere, my hair filthy and standing up in spikes where I had run my hands through it, and my breath smelling of brandy.

Especially the breath part. Booze was something Ben, my ex-husband, had made a big deal of when we'd been married. But we all have our ways of coping, and a little alcohol to lighten the pain had been mine. He had just shut down, avoiding all emotional contact while we both grieved for Becky, each in our own way, shut off in our own little misery boxes.

But right now, all I could see on his face was pity, and I think that might have been worse than anything else. I turned away quickly, but not before he saw the tears in my eyes.

"Gracie, listen—is there somewhere we can go to talk? Your place wasn't damaged in the fire, was it?"

"No, the house my great-grandparents built is still standing solid a century later—a little smoke-stained but still safe." A bit like Ben's arms…strong and safe.

I quickly shook that last thought from my head.

Ben mistook the reaction, and his mouth tightened. "I just want to get a statement from you, and I thought your house would be a better spot than that noisy hall."

I wasn't trying to get you into bed was his subtext. I'd gotten good at reading subtexts with Ben—and I knew damn well he wasn't interested in getting me into bed. I sniffed, anger and hurt straightening my spine, and marched down the street towards home.

****

"How are you, Gracie?" Ben's voice was gentle, with that special timbre that had once made me go all soft inside. *Once. But not now.*

But as I gazed at my ex-husband across the kitchen table, I knew I wasn't fooling myself. I still loved Ben. Pity there was a mountain range of stumbling blocks to keep us apart. *Don't go there, Gracie. Don't think of Becky now.*

"I guess I'm as well as anyone else in Jacques Station—better than most, actually. My house is still standing. But I was up all night with everyone else…did you know we formed an old-fashioned bucket chain to bring water from the mill pond and put out small fires?"

"Oh—look at your hands!"

I hadn't noticed the pain until that moment, but it hit me when I looked down at my open palms. I'd been talking with my hands again—not a good thing for a counselor, too distracting for the client—and Ben had paled under his summer tan as he'd seen the red meat that my hands had become. Blisters had formed on blisters as we passed buckets of water, then the blisters had burst and bled, and on top of that, I'd fallen on red hot rocks and scorched my palms when I'd found…

Suddenly the memory was too much. Tears flowed from my eyes without my permission, making grey tracks though the soot and muck on my face.

"Gracie…"

I turned away, waving one throbbing hand at him in a "keep away" gesture. But I couldn't stop the tears, and when Ben put his arms around me, I turned and sobbed into his jacket.

He mumbled words into my hair, and the mumbling turned to kisses, and without meaning to, I raised my mouth to his. He captured it, first nibbling at my lips and then deepening the kiss as he felt my response…and then I was back five years. No, more, to when our love had still been sweet and new and we'd explored every inch of each other, body and mind, at every opportunity.

Ben groaned softly, pressing me to him even more

tightly. Feeling him harden in response inflamed me, the old aching longing that had been tamped down now threatening to burst into flame as my body, heart, and soul wanted to blend with his.

And then the door flew open and the McDonagh family—Mom, Pop and two teenaged sons—stood there in a shocked silence. They were backlighted by the morning sun, but I'm pretty sure I could have guessed at their expressions, and "surprised" would be a mild way of putting it.

"Oh, sorry to disturb you, Gracie! Er, if you're busy, we can come back another..."

"Sandy, no, it's okay. Inspector Pelham and I were just talking."

"Talking?"

"Yes, about the fire and the body..."

"Looked more like he was giving her mouth-to-mouth resuscitation," one of the sons, Jacko, whispered to his sibling, and the other snickered, sparking murder in my heart, but a quick glance at Ben showed an impassive, official police expression. I wanted to kick him.

"You said we could bunk with you for a day or two, and it would be so much better than the motel in Kingston they're suggesting we stay in...you know, for work and the school bus and everything..." Mac McDonagh stammered.

"Just until we can sort something else out..." his wife, Sandy, added, with a knowing grin. "But if it's inconvenient...the bus for the motels is leaving in half an hour."

I crossed the room quickly and hugged her, taking the opportunity to whisper in her ear, "If you or any of your family breathe a word about this, losing your house will be the least of your worries."

"Oh, I do understand you so completely," she gushed back at me, and I could see she was really enjoying herself. I considered crossing her off my Christmas card list, but instead offered to take them upstairs and show them the two bedrooms they could use.

"There's a bathroom upstairs between the bedrooms, and another one ensuite in my room, so you can shower if you want. Towels are in the closet at the head of the stairs, and clean sheets are in the blanket boxes in each bedroom. Just make yourself at home, help yourself to whatever you need in the kitchen. I'll put the coffeemaker on," I chattered brightly as I showed them around, leaving them upstairs to settle themselves.

"Why, you're a proper little hostess, aren't you? Ever thought of opening a B'n'B?" Ben said sarcastically as I busied myself back in the kitchen, putting on coffee and checking the fridge for milk—and trying hard not to meet his eyes.

"Frankly, I was glad of the interruption," I said finally, sitting down at the table and placing two mugs of coffee in front of us. "What just happened should never happen again."

Ben's face closed, but his eyes were sharp as he watched me.

"You wanted to speak to me about something? I'm assuming your visit had some other purpose than opening up a past that should be kept locked?"

Ben's scowl deepened. "I'm not investigating the cause of the fire. That's up to the fire marshal's office and then local police or the RCMP. I was called in to investigate the unexplained death of the person—presumed to be a young man—found at the feed store."

"And you want to know how I came to stumble across a dead body?"

"It's getting to be kind of a habit of yours."

I scowled at him, but his statement had been factual rather than malicious. About a year ago I'd been involved in a local theatre production of a new play when a cast member went missing. I didn't exactly stumble over the body; it was more like it fell on me—from the props. Dr Flynne's death certainly made the opening night memorable, and probably killed my writing career in its infancy.

"I don't need the commentary, thank you very much. Okay, all that happened was, as it started to come light and the fire was under control, I sat on my front stoop to get my breath—I was dog tired after not sleeping all night, and all the bucket chain work…"

"I can understand that…"

"Thank you. Anyway, Alex McGeary came and sat with me, and we were chatting—he's an old friend from when we were kids, and he's also the village reeve…" I was gabbling now; I do that when I'm bone weary. And when I'm with Ben. "So anyway, Millie—that's Mildred Cairns—she's eighty-nine if she's a day, and probably showing the first signs of senile dementia… Anyway, she came along calling for Maxie. She couldn't find him…"

"Maxie? Could that be the name of the victim?"

"No, no—Maxie's her cat. But to Millie, he's all the family she's got, and she loves him. She was calling for him and crying and seemed pretty disoriented. Anyway, I couldn't let her wander around the smoldering buildings on her own—she'd probably have been toasted herself—so I took her arm and went with her. We heard a meowing down the side alley alongside the feed store, and spotted Maxie cowering up in a corner, obviously terrified. Millie bolted in to get him, and I followed her. I was really afraid she'd be hurt. I managed to get her and the cat and pointed her in the direction of the street, and then I tripped and fell over…over something. That's when I burned my hands on some hot cement blocks…and when I looked down to see what I'd tripped over, it was…it was…"

Ben reached over and covered my hand with his. "Okay, now, do you have any idea who it might be?"

"I was talking to Rev Allie Spence at the United Church, in the hall, just before I met you, and she said everyone seemed to be accounted for but some of the township kids had been here for a baseball game last night and she was wondering if it…if he was one of them. She was going to phone around to make sure everyone had gotten home safely. She's probably the best person to talk to."

Ben nodded. "Has there been any trouble around here recently? Any gangs? Maybe drugs?"

I looked at him, wide-eyed. "Are you kidding? Probably half the village has a few maryjane plants tucked among the trees, and some people take it further than a hobby. This is one of the last refuges for the old hippies, after all. To say nothing of there being no jobs to speak of and everyone looking to make a few bucks, especially when the city people visit."

"Is it worth bringing in a task force?"

I wasn't sure if he was serious or not. "Do that, and you'll probably get me strung up from the gantry they use down at the Legion for the deer-weighing contest every fall."

"Well, we wouldn't want anything like that to happen, would we? Is there anything else you can think of?"

I shook my head, and he closed his notebook. "Gracie...when we parted the last time, I know you said you didn't want to see me again, but..."

"Hey, Dr. Pelham! We're really hungry. Anything in the fridge—oh, sorry, are we interrupting again?"

I made a mental note to kill the McDonagh teens one dark night. Then shuddered, because someone had obviously killed one young man already, in the alleyway across from my home.

Ben and I carried out the rest of our conversation in a stiff, formal manner under the smirking grins of the two boys as they proceeded to raid the contents of my refrigerator and kitchen cupboards.

"Hey, you've got nothing but yoghurt and fruit and cheese and stuff in here—don't you have any real food?" Jacko complained.

Well, yes, I do have my own stash of junk food, but there is no way I'm sharing it with you kids. Call me selfish. After much sighing and slamming of cupboard doors, the pair finally disappeared back to the television upstairs, clutching a mound of peanut butter and banana sandwiches and looking thoroughly put-upon. "Yuk—it's all-wheat bread," I heard the smaller one mutter as they left.

"It's supposed to be good for you," the bigger one replied with a shudder. "Mom will be so pleased."

"Who'd have thought Dr. Pelham was like Mom? I thought she was way cool."

I ignored Ben's grin and looked at my watch—
damn! I had a late afternoon therapy group at one of the
halfway houses in Kingston, and I didn't want to cry off
despite the bone weariness that was engulfing my body
and mind.

"You're still trying to redeem those rapists and child
abusers, Gracie?"

"It's my job. It's what I'm trained for," I snapped.

"But we all know why you really do it, don't we?
And it won't work, Gracie. If every police force, every
social worker in the country is still looking, what makes
you think you can pull the rabbit out of the hat? You
really think that one of the perverts you work with would
lift a finger to help you?"

My fingers itched to smack that scorn off his face,
but I resisted. Why give him the satisfaction of knowing
his words had hit home?

"Go to hell, Ben." That was the best I could do. And
I left him sitting there in my country kitchen, taking a
last gulp of coffee from a mug emblazoned with
chickens. When I came back downstairs, dressed in a
white blouse and navy-blue pants suit, sensible shoes on
my feet, Ben was gone.

I didn't know whether I wanted to laugh or cry.

Chapter Three

"I heard you had quite a to-do up there in Jacques Station," John Haggarty, supervisor of the halfway house for ex-cons, said to me as he showed me into the therapy room. "I wasn't expecting you to show up today at all."

"Funnily enough, I was hoping dealing with our clients might take my mind off the horror I left behind."

John grinned. "Good luck with that!"

I wriggled out of my heavy winter coat and stowed it and my purse in one of the lockers, being careful to turn the key so that no one could access the contents. "It was bad, John—the fire has destroyed a lot of homes and damaged quite a few more. It might be the end of the village, frankly—the place was hardly getting by as it was, and now there'll be a few people leaving rather than rebuilding, if they owned, or because the homes they've been renting are burned out and they've got to go somewhere else."

"It's sad, so many of the small communities are going under—and the increased cost of gas is going to make it so much worse," Haggarty said. "I've a couple of guys who live here at the halfway house and have jobs in the townships, and frankly, they can barely afford to work at the rates of pay they get, not when they have the cost of traveling."

"And without jobs to keep them steady and give them a work record, they'll wind up back in jail as repeat offenders," I said. "It's an old pattern come back again with a new cover."

"Guess it keeps us in jobs though, doesn't it?" He smiled ruefully.

"Not a comforting thought, that," I said, gathering a pile of manila-colored folders from the cubbyhole with my name on it in magic marker.

"You've got a new guy in the group today—Seth Marshall. Two-time offender—likes little girls and isn't showing a lot of remorse but he's done his time, so I guess we'll see what happens with him." John didn't sound all that hopeful, but every time I got a new client in the therapy group, I experienced a little shiver of hope.

That hope itself was a contradiction in terms. These were men who liked to have sex with children. The ones who interested me the most hurt little girls.

Little girls like my Becky. Ben's child, my daughter. Becky had run skipping from my car over four years ago, dressed in her new pink dungarees and striped sox, off to a friend's birthday party in a local park. I'd watched until she reached the gaily decorated picnic tables where the other kids were already getting hyper on junk food, then waved and left for work.

That was the last time we saw our daughter. Becky was playing hide and seek with the other kids and apparently went off to hide in the woods. No one knew what happened to her after that. How can one small child disappear without a trace?

Which brings me back to my interest in these men, the sort of people most members of the public would rather believe didn't exist. But I saw each of them as a possible gateway into a community that was shunned by "normal" people, but tightly knit. These men knew how little girls could be made to disappear. One day, I hoped, one of them would show me how to bring my little Becky home.

Dead or alive.

****

Seth Marshall was a man who'd stand out in any crowd, quite literally. The man was six-foot-six if he was an inch, with shoulders like a buffalo on steroids and a shock of black hair that hung in a ponytail down his back. His skin was swarthy but with the pale tones of a man who hasn't spent much time in the sunlight in recent years. But his eyes were piercing, intent, and I had to repress a little shiver when his gaze touched me.

A shiver of what? Apprehension? Recognition? Fear? Attraction?

Well, probably not a lot of point in being attracted to a man who, according to his file, had just put in eight years in the pen for molesting a young child. Clearly, I wasn't his type.

And if I was afraid of him, I had to nip that in the bud. Let these guys get a hint of fear, especially from a female authority figure, and they'd be all over me like a poison ivy rash.

"Okay, everybody, can we all settle down please? We've a new group member today. Say hello to Seth Marshall, guys."

The seven or eight other men in the room speared Seth with their eyes, with one exception: Joey Clarke. Joey never looked anyone in the eye. Ever.

Some of the others managed a grunt of welcome, but Seth seemed unimpressed, one way or the other.

"Okay, Mr. Marshall, as the new guy in the group, perhaps you'd like to tell us a little about yourself?"

"Like what?" His voice was surprisingly light for a man of his size.

"Well, we know your name and the fact that you're living in this halfway house. Where are you from? What work do you do? How long were you in prison? And where do you hope to go from here?"

He challenged me with those intense eyes, but I wouldn't back down. In the end he sighed and said, "I'm an auto mechanic, I spent eight wonderful years in the pen, and as for where I'd like to go from here—a child's birthday party in the park would be great."

His words froze me. I couldn't respond to the whooping and hollering of some of the other guys, who thought Seth's ambitions were delightful. I could only stare at his knowing expression and wonder if this was just a lucky shot or if he knew my daughter had been abducted from a party in the park. Was he trying to tell me something, or was he just screwing with me?

I deliberately looked away and spent a few moments writing something in my notepad, for all the world as if I were making notes about Seth to be used against him at a later date. Two can play the intimidation game.

By the time I looked up, the other guys were quieted down, slouched in their seats, and staring at the ground. All except Seth, who was still trying to psych me out.

"I'm going to ignore that comment for now, Mr. Marshall. This is your first time at group. But another crack like that and I'll have to report it to your guidance officer—and you may find your parole will be revoked. Now, does anyone have anything they would like to say to the group?"

A few moments' silence passed, and then I winced as a little bespectacled man jumped to his feet. Richard

Bonner—Tricky Dicky to his friends—loved the limelight and would speak for the entire therapy session if I let him.

"I just wanted to say that I've been thinking a lot about my life, and first of all, I think it's very wrong that a man is pilloried for loving children. Me, I'd never hurt a kid. I love them. Now I'm ordered to stay away from anywhere there are children, and all the time there are crackheads and whores out there, popping out babies and torturing them and prostituting them…"

"Hey, Dicky, do you have an address for one of these crackhead whores, maybe with a nice little ten-year-old daughter?" An older man, Jason Pelligrew, tittered at his own joke. Again, I did the note writing intimidatory thing, and silence eventually fell.

"Anyone other than Mr. Bonner have anything they want to say?"

"I've been feeling very depressed the last few days." The quiet little guy in the back row actually spoke up. He'd been so quiet I couldn't remember him really speaking before.

"Why do you think that is, Lyle?"

Lyle Richmond was a little mustachioed man who rarely spoke at these sessions. He usually seemed intimidated by the others, and even his crime had been at arm's length—he had been caught with a computer full of kiddie-porn. I doubted Lyle had ever had a close relationship in his life—not surprising, when I considered his background notes in the case file.

"I…I just have this feeling that I don't belong anywhere, and I can't sleep at night. I keep thinking of the things I've done…and I'm sure that no one likes me."

"Ya got that right, fella!" Pelligrew, rapidly earning

his place as class clown, guffawed. The others followed suit, but my glare quelled them.

"All of you, mark this. One of the rules for your release has been that you live at this halfway house and that you attend therapy sessions. One of the rules of the therapy session is that each person is treated with respect, not subjected to ridicule or threat. Give a guess what happens if you're thrown out of the therapy sessions?"

That got them quieted, but try as I might, I couldn't get Lyle to speak again, let alone open up. I made a quick note on my notebook to ask John Haggarty if I could do some one-to-one sessions with Lyle. There was something about the little man that worried me. The man had not mentioned suicidal thoughts, but his words and general appearance suggested them.

Then, to my relief, the session was over. I'd learned nothing, other than that counseling those who for the most part didn't want to be counseled was like pushing a snowball uphill in the desert. You never achieved your goal and just ended up looking all wet. But then, I'd already learned that lesson.

****

The rest of my hours at Halton House for ex-cons was taken up with a staff conference and paperwork, paperwork, paperwork. By the time I'd written up my own notes and filed them, it was well into the evening, and I was about ready to go home and sleep. I saw my boss, John Haggarty, putting on his jacket, ready to leave, and cornered him to ask about the individual sessions for Lyle.

"I doubt there's enough left in the funding pot for individual sessions," he said. "We're short of funds as it is, trying to do more with less all the time. What's bothering you about Lyle?"

"Just that he seems to be going through some sort of crisis. He actually worked up the courage to speak in therapy group today—and was shot down by the new boy, Seth Marshall. He's a real work of art. But I'm afraid Lyle may be getting to a stage where he either talks or tries to end it all. He's very much a depressive."

Haggarty scrubbed his face with his hands. He looked tired but working with cons and ex-cons will do that for you. "Lord, we certainly don't want a suicide or some other incident here, not after the bad publicity there's been for halfway houses—or early release programs for sex offenders. Listen, Gracie, leave it with me and I'll see what I can do."

I had to be content with that, but I wasn't going to hold my breath. It was unlikely that the government would loosen the purse strings for my kind of work in the corrections services any time soon. I'd do some pro-bono work with Lyle if necessary, because I was so concerned—but that's a slippery slope. Give free therapy sessions to one, and before you know it, there's a queue of needy/manipulative cases at your door.

****

My cell phone gave a cheery little chirrup just as I was getting into my car.

"Gracie, I'm so glad I caught you," Allie said, sounding breathless. "I just wanted to know if we were still on for tonight?"

"You want to go ahead with the Girls Night In, despite the village being almost burned to the ground?"

"Hey, lots of places posted We Never Closed signs during the London Blitz, so why can't we do the same? Besides, we all need to relax. Will you be there? My place?"

"I don't know, Allie. Will Tina be there? I'm kind of beat—today's been my therapy group with the boys in Kingston, and I'm not up to another little scene like the one Tina pulled in the hall."

Allie took a deep breath and let it out. "I am so sorry about that, Gracie. She doesn't really mean anything by it, she's just very insecure…"

"Yeah, right. And mean as a scrapyard dog, to boot." I was sorry as soon as I spoke the words, but there was no taking them back.

"Perhaps it would be better to cancel the Girl's Night In tonight. I guess everyone is strung out."

I wasn't sure whether I was more annoyed at Allie's unspoken defense of Tina or at her dismissal of my feelings as just being strung out like everyone else. Although maybe there was some truth to it. Even so, I ended the call in a snit.

Of course, after a two-hour drive during which my head pounded and my stomach—or an incipient ulcer— repeatedly reminded me that I'd missed lunch, who should I find on my doorstep back in Jacques Station but Ben, my soon-to-be ex-husband? Could my day get any worse?

Irritably, I opened the old wooden storm door on the heavy front door. I paused for a moment and couldn't stifle a yawn, hoping against hope that Ben would take the hint and suggest he'd come back tomorrow. Or never.

"Let me guess—you were in the area and thought you'd drop in for afternoon tea?" He probably didn't deserve the sarcastic greeting, but I was tired, discouraged, and not in the mood to make nice to the man I loved but couldn't stand being around.

"Actually, we've got an ID on the body you discovered at the feed store."

My heart sank. Not more bad news. "Who was it? One of the local boys?"

"Can we go inside?" he said finally. We'd been standing on the concrete stoop outside my front door, with me partially blocking the access in a not-too-subtle but unconscious statement that I didn't want to invite him in. I tried not to show my reluctance to let Ben enter my home and instead shrugged as if it didn't matter. But when I tried to get the key in the lock to open the heavy maple front door, my hands were shaking, and I couldn't get the key and the lock together.

Was it Ben's nearness, or was it the possibility that he was about to reveal the death of a young man I knew that caused my hands to shake?

Ben took the key from me and quickly mated the key with the lock, and moments later we were standing in my dim hallway. Trying to put off hearing his news for a few moments longer, I walked down the hallway, past the stately center stairway that curved upwards with an elegance that reflected the era in which the house had been built. I heard his footsteps behind me but didn't look at him as I flicked on the light switch above the antique pine table in the center of the room and then held the kettle under the faucet to fill it for tea.

Ben did that chewing-the-bottom-lip thing that meant he was trying to decide what to say. Another of his little habits I knew so well and found so annoying. He'd followed me into the room and now leaned his tall frame against the old-fashioned refrigerator.

Without being asked, he seemed to reach a decision and sat down at the round kitchen table with its blue woven placemats depicting an inexplicably cheery country duck. Irritated at his presumption—okay, I know it was ridiculous, but that's how it was between Ben and me—I slammed the kettle down and switched it on. "I'm making tea. The last thing either of us needs is to be kept awake by caffeine."

But when I turned to put mugs on the table, I caught a glimpse of Ben's face and sucked in a shocked breath. He was grey with exhaustion, his eyes momentarily closed as if he was relaxing for the first time in a very long time.

My irrational irritation vanished like melting ice in the face of spring's first warm breeze, and I sat down opposite him.

"Ben, you look exhausted. Why don't you take a break and just have a cup of tea before you say anything else?"

His eyes opened, their piercing blue gaze as always looking right through to my soul. At least, that's how it seemed.

"It's been a long day, Gracie. You must be pretty beat yourself. I'll just run this by you and be on my way so you can get to bed," he said, and our eyes locked as we both thought of the happier times we'd gone to bed together...

But Ben was the first to recover, and he was all business. Police business.

"The body discovered in the alley alongside the feed store was, as you're aware, very badly burned. However, we've managed to identify him as male, about twenty-four years old, about five foot six inches tall, and probably having had a broken arm at some point in the past.

"While it's too soon to be sure, and not all the tests are back yet, it seems the subject matches the description of a young man reported missing by his mother after he didn't come home. He was last seen on Saturday evening."

"That doesn't sound like anyone local," I said, feeling unworthy that hope was threaded through my voice.

"No, he's from just north of Jamesville, a young man by the name of Ralph Morris."

"Ralph Morris?" I felt almost giddy.

"Yeah, apparently his mother prided herself as being a fashionista and, with her own last name being Morris, thought it only proper to pay tribute to a great fashion designer by naming her son after him."

God forgive me, the poor guy was dead and I felt like laughing at his name. To hide that, I got up and went to the now boiling kettle, filling the teapot with hot water over tea bags and bringing the works back to the table.

"So it seems pretty conclusive that this young man is Ralph Morris?" I asked. "Do you know what he was doing up here in Jacques Station? Was he visiting someone local?"

"That's a possibility. We know there are a lot of marijuana farmers up here, so perhaps he was buying stock."

"He was a drug dealer?"

"He'd already served time as a youth for dealing and possession, everything from crack to simple hash, and looked about set to do another stretch, this time in adult incarceration, the way he was going on."

"Do you have a cause of death yet? Was it the fire?"

"No, Gracie. It looks like Mr. Morris died Saturday

evening. He'd apparently been stabbed multiple times."

I shivered, thinking of that poor boy lying just a few hundred yards away from my home, dying, and no one had known.

Except the killer.

"So what aren't you telling me, Ben?"

Ben's face turned a little greyer with tiredness as he reached for a cup and poured himself tea. I knew he was just playing for time while he got his thoughts together, and I busied myself pouring tea for myself from the pretty teapot I'd found at a thrift store. It had tiny kittens gamboling along the sides and…

"We've had other known drug dealers killed in Frontenac County recently. All young men. All the same way. And no one has seen or heard anything." The frustration in Ben's voice was palpable.

We drank tea in silence for a little while. I thought Ben was going to elaborate on what he thought might be going on, but at that moment we were interrupted in a flurry of parents, teenaged kids, and grocery bags of various sizes.

The McDonagh family had arrived back at their temporary digs in my home, in a whirlwind of chatter and teenage grumbling, take-out pizza smells, and tired parental rebukes.

I did a quick introduction, something I'd neglected earlier, explaining to Ben that their rented home had suffered a lot of damage and was no longer habitable, and they were to stay with me for few days.

"I have lots of space in this old house," I told anyone who was listening. Ben shook hands with the parents, smiled at the boys, and thanked me for the tea.

"Keep safe, and please keep our conversation to

yourself. Call me if there's any news," he said, and left me to deal with the exhausted McDonaghs.

Ben was headed for the motel rooms assigned to the out-of-town detectives investigating the fire and others investigating the murder of Ralph Morris. Also in the motel was a games room now acting as a police incident room they'd set up in the motel on highway seven. At least Lucy MacAllister, who ran the failing motel, would gain something from all this.

I quickly showed my guests where they could stash their food and drinks that they'd brought, where to find pots and pans and dish towels, and then left them to work up some meals in the kitchen.

When they were settled and the hungry teens were busy making steady inroads into the huge takeaway pizzas they'd brought, I decided to clear my head by taking the dog, Josh, for a walk.

Actually, the sweet pooch isn't mine but belongs to my next-door neighbor, Katie Swartz. Katie was recovering from a badly twisted ankle after a fall on the rough pavement on our street and was happy to have me take the pooch for some exercise.

It was a lovely night, the darkness a deep velvet punctuated by stars that twinkled brightly like a nursery rhyme. The pooch and I took a long run along the now disused CN rail track. The dog was delighted, but my heart was still heavy as I dropped her back to her owner and returned to my own home as the night was closing in.

****

The ringing of my doorbell dragged me from a mixed-up dream of being attacked by a giant marshmallow while walking on a beach with that yummy

Horatio from *CSI Miami*. Turned out I'd fallen asleep in front of the TV, but one part of my mind must have been still tuned in to the television and registering the CSI's war against crime.

The bell went right on ringing—whoever was there had stuck their thumb on it and wasn't taking it off anytime soon—unless the batteries on the wireless device gave out. And somehow, I didn't think I'd be that lucky.

So, rubbing the sleep from my eyes, I crossed the living room into the dining room and peeked through the glass of the Victorian front door to see who my visitor was. My friend Reverend Allie. My anger and sense of betrayal at her words earlier were forgotten as I pulled the door open and saw her sheepish smile and the bottle of cheap wine she held out.

"Peace offering?"

"You could say that. I felt terrible about the fight we had on the phone and figured you could use a drink as much as I could." Rev Allie stepped into my home and shook off raindrops that bejeweled her frizzy dark hair.

"I didn't realize it was raining. It would have been great to dampen the fire that did so much damage, if we'd had it that night."

Rev. Allie smiled, but her eyes were serious as she followed me into the kitchen. Fortunately, the McDonagh family had eaten and retired to their rooms, so I took a frozen pizza out of the freezer—my stomach was telling me I hadn't eaten much since this morning's toast.

"Like some? It's not a giant marshmallow, but then, you're not Horatio." I grinned at her, enjoying the look of puzzlement on her face before I told her of my dream.

She laughed. "Sounds like you were having an interesting evening until I woke you up."

And, just like that, the tension was gone. Allie and I had been friends since I'd been a summer kid here and she was the daughter of the local minister. We'd run in a wild gang together, grazing at each other's homes and getting up to all sorts of mischief that today's kids were too protected to even dream about.

I said as much to Allie as we waited for the pizza and sipped at the sharp red wine she'd brought. It was plonk in the worst way, but also good in the way that any wine drunk with friends is good.

"Yes, kids today don't have anywhere near the freedom that we had—our parents wouldn't have been calling the police if they didn't see us until dark, and the things we did! Remember the time we tried to build a raft? We took that bit of hardboard out onto the lake, eight of us, and the thing sank!"

"Yeah, good thing we were all strong swimmers— no life jackets or safety equipment in those days."

"Yet, in many ways, it's a much more dangerous world for children now."

"You're thinking of the young man who was killed here on Saturday?" I pulled the pizza out of the oven, already feeling my appetite diminishing.

"The rumor around town is that he was a drug dealer—sold hash to little kids, then got them on crack."

I could hear the question mark at the end of Allie's sentence. She knew—as did the entire village by now— that Ben had visited. She was no doubt wondering if I had any news to quieten the fears that had sprung up. People were keeping their children indoors—the ones who still had homes—and the rest were debating whether they'd ever be comfortable to return to Jacques Station after the fire and the murder.

"Ben didn't tell me much, if that's what you're wondering. He did say that the boy was probably a drug dealer—sounds like that's common knowledge. But he was so young—Ben showed me a picture. His mother must be heartbroken…"

"And so must the mothers of all the kids who've suffered because he was making a few bucks out of them." Allie's voice was laced with bitterness.

I took another swallow of the wine. It tasted even more bitter now. "Allie, I know you see so much of the grief that this stuff causes, but you must remember this boy was probably a hurt creature, too."

Allie sighed. "It sounds like our roles have been reversed—you're the mild-mannered church minister, and I'm the cynical psychologist."

"Won't do any harm to have a change of viewpoint. We both, in our own ways, see a lot of suffering."

So we spent the rest of the late evening eating pizza and drinking bad wine, Allie sprawled over my sofa and me sitting on the rug with my back to a chair. It was just like old times. For one brief moment I cursed Tina for the wedge she tried to drive between Allie and me. I opened my mouth to speak, and thought better of it, so we watched a couple of mindless sitcoms, laughing at things the writers never intended to be funny, did some girl-chat bonding, and finally, both dog tired, we called it a night, friends again.

But when I went to bed that night, I realized that once upon a time I would have told her anything I knew, even told her information Ben had said I shouldn't share with anyone.

That three young men had died. All in the same brutal way.

Three is three too many, especially in the rural Land o' Lakes area, where violent death was blessedly rare indeed, except for fatal car crashes in the tourist season or during some of the ice and heavy snowstorms we had. These boys may have been drug dealers—among the lowest of the social pond scum—but drug dealing isn't a death penalty crime under Canadian law.

And I couldn't get out of my head the idea that a young man had lain so close to my home one night, dying, and I'd probably been glued to the TV, or working on my laptop, or fast asleep, completely unaware of his suffering.

But now another thought crept into my mind and chased sleep away for a long time.

Three apparently related deaths meant that a killer with no conscience, a psychopath, could be on the loose in our quiet little neighborhood. Worse, that someone who was killing these young dealers probably thought they were ridding the world of evil.

That thought kept sleep from coming for a long time that night.

Chapter Four

The morning dawned bright and sunny, not that I saw much of it. After a sleepless night, I greeted the ringing of my alarm clock by pulling the covers over my head and finally falling into a deep, dreamless sleep. I was too tired to throw the damned thing across the room, and I think it realized what a narrow escape it had had, because it remained quiet for the next couple of hours.

I'd been grateful for healing the rift with Allie, yet the laughter and wine hadn't helped me sleep. In fact, it felt like only a rather delicate peace had descended. It was quite the opposite to our tell-all, total support, pre-Tina friendship. I'd tossed and turned well into the night, thinking about the dead boy who'd lain across from my house, unnoticed until the fire. Of lost life and joy. And finally, of Becky.

I'd cried myself to sleep.

At some time in the early morning, I heard the clatter of teenaged feet and the shushing of parents as the whole McDonagh family left for some unknown destination.

When I next woke up, it was to a brutal headache and a continuous ringing that tempted me to make good on my threat to toss the poor alarm clock against the wall and then put my head back under the covers. The ringing continued, and finally I had to acknowledge the sound was actually coming from the doorbell. Pulling on my favorite silk dressing gown—a retail therapy item bought

43

for my own pleasure after signing divorce papers for Ben—I stepped carefully down the gracious stairs, knowing full well I wasn't anything like the vision of ladylike elegance that the original owners and builders had envisaged.

That damned bell was still ringing when I finally arrived at the door. Some people simply cannot take a hint and go away. I yanked the door open with something less than grace.

Jack Lennon stood there, clutching a large bunch of gas station flowers and wearing a super-compassionate look on his face. Which, to his credit, slipped only slightly when he saw the state of me.

"Gracie—I was thinking about you and the troubles of Jacques Station, and knew you'd need a little support and cheering up…"

Support and cheering up was something of an understatement, I told him, pointing towards the kitchen and following him there.

"So how do you feel about everything?" he said, laying the flowers down on the table and moving to fill the coffee pot.

"You know, Jack, right now that question has me grinding my teeth. How the hell would anyone feel when most of their neighborhood has been incinerated, longtime friends are faced with moving somewhere else, and a dead body was lying across the street from me and I did nothing to help?"

Jack stood with his mouth open. That gave me some sense of satisfaction, which my ego immediately converted to shame. Jack is my supervising therapist—the therapist's therapist, if you see what I mean. Most counselors have someone in the trade that they check in with every few weeks or so, laying on that person's shoulders all the detritus accumulated through hours of listening to the pain, the anger, the sometime lies, the horror of clients who come to us seeking peace.

Jack had listened to me many times; he'd heard my complaints, my rants, my fears that I was unable to help a client in need. During the dreadful time when a client had committed suicide, Jack was the one who sat with me while I wailed and cried and berated first myself and then the client. Jack was also the one who held my head while I vomited a pint of whisky out into the toilet, but I'd rather not dwell on that inglorious moment.

"Sorry, Jack. I had a tough therapy group yesterday, then a fight with my best friend—and to complete the day, my ex-husband is the cop in charge of the investigation..." I almost said "murder investigation" but remembered in time that Ben had told me to keep mum, so I did a quick verbal bypass.

But mention of Ben was enough to distract Jack. One day soon I was going to have to do something about my relationship with my supervisor. Or, rather, his relationship with me, because there was little doubt that Jack had growing feelings for me that were less and less appropriate as time went by.

Which explains his increasing antipathy and tendency to criticize my almost ex-husband at every chance he got.

"I thought we'd already discussed how you needed to protect yourself by staying away from your ex and keeping him at arm's length. You look like you didn't sleep, which is what happens to you every time he's around." Jack dropped the flowers onto the antique pine kitchen table, his look saying more than words could about how he felt about my behavior.

I took a deep breath, feeling like a schoolgirl called before the principal to answer for some careless youthful indiscretion. And you certainly couldn't describe my relationship with Ben as a careless youthful indiscretion. Childish, yes, but neither youthful nor careless. Besides which, it had damn all to do with Jack.

I busied myself with setting the coffee maker going and then laying out mugs, cream, milk, and sugar. I did not want my overtired mind to snap at Jack, because he is a good friend and a co-worker, after all.

"Ben was here in an official capacity, Jack. I was the one who found the body, so I was high on his list for questioning." I didn't mention that Ben had visited twice, nor the heat that sprang between us every time we were in the same room.

Jack got up and busied himself pouring coffee and adding the accoutrements, his back to me and his face hidden. It never dawned on him that it might be impolite to presume that he had kitchen rights, but I was too much at a disadvantage, standing here close to noon in my silk robe, with my hair standing out in all directions and my eyes still swollen with sleep.

I jumped when the bell rang again, spilling coffee from the mug Jack handed me.

Like Union Station, my house some days.

But the train now waiting at Platform One was none other than my almost-ex, who took in my sleepy eyed, just-out-of-bed appearance and the slinky silk gown with something approaching appreciation on his face. I scowled at him as I let him enter through the front door.

And then Jack called from the kitchen. "Gracie, love, come and get this coffee while it's fresh, and I'll rustle us up some breakfast."

Ben's eyes went hard, and that lovely melting look that had me mesmerized turned to ice. "You have company?"

"Jack—you've met Jack, I think—my supervising counselor?" Of course, he had—like the last time he walked unexpectedly into my kitchen and found Jack embracing me…

"Supervising? Is that what you call it? I thought you told me there was nothing between the two of you?"

"That's it, okay? Anyway, it's nothing to do with you who's in my kitchen—or in my bed, if it comes to that," I snapped, cheeks growing pink. "You sent me the divorce papers, remember? You were the one who wanted a clean break, a fresh start, and multiple other cliches."

And I slammed the door in his face.

"Who was that?" Jack asked, coming towards me down the hallway with a large mug of coffee in his hand.

"No one important," I said loudly. Then the doorbell rang again.

"Can't you take a hint and get lost?" I shouted, yanking the door open.

Instead of an irritating ex-husband, my first client of the morning stood there.

"Mrs. LeBlanc! Maria! I wasn't expecting you! I mean, after the fire and everything that's happened. Did no one contact you?"

I wished with all my heart that antique rug in my hallway would rise up and swallow me whole, I was so embarrassed as the older lady eyed my silk robe and took in the man standing behind me in the kitchen doorway, clutching coffee and looking well at home.

"I gather from your state of dress that you weren't expecting me, Dr. Gracie. However, no self-respecting, money-hungry shrink would tell a $225 date to take a hike," and Maria swept into my home with a disapproving glance towards the kitchen and the man standing there holding a coffeepot, then made a beeline for the office I used at home.

I hurried into the kitchen, grabbed a coffee, and rolled my eyes at Jack as I returned to my client.

"Just give me a few moments to make myself look a bit more professional," I told Maria LeBlanc, to much eye-rolling from her. I dashed upstairs and found pants and a shirt, slipped my feet into sandals, and pulled a brush through my sleep-tangled hair. In an amazingly short time, I was back down the stairs and heading towards my office and the irritated client waiting there.

"I'll maybe drop by later," Jack said to my back.

I hesitated and then turned. "Maybe that's not such a good idea, Jack. I need to catch up on a lot of work, and I need to do some thinking."

"Yeah, and could you maybe do that on your own time, not mine? The clock's ticking, Dr. Gracie." Maria's voice carried from the back of the house with a sound like gravel scraping on cement. I rolled my eyes again and hurried to the office, but I didn't relax until I heard the front door close behind Jack.

"You, young lady, are getting far too tied up in men. Seems they're in and out of here like you're handing out…well, never mind. Can't you just settle down with that handsome husband of yours and leave some guys for the rest of us?"

Marie has some relationship issues and seems to want to make up in the sexual Olympics in her sixties what she'd been too repressed to enjoy in her twenties. That's why she was seeing me. And a conversation with her was the last thing I needed right now.

Okay, Gracie, steel yourself—it's only for another forty goddamn minutes!

"And stop looking at your watch—my straightlaced son is paying for this time, not that I understand what the problem is. Just because I developed a friendship with that cute little gardener..."

The "gardener" was probably barely legal age. *Oh, my God!* "I take it you're talking about Richard DeGeert—the high school student you hired to prune your roses," I said.

"If that's what you want to call it, dear." She looked like the cat who'd just enjoyed fun and games with a canary...

Oh, dear God, get me out of here...

Maria's fifty minutes passed with dragging feet, but finally it was over. I felt a twinge of guilt that I hadn't been a lot of use as her counselor today, but I quickly excused myself on the grounds that she shouldn't have been here at all—the joint office staff who took care of my appointments and messages had called my clients and cancelled everything for the rest of the week, barring an emergency.

But Maria, who didn't believe she was subject to the rules the rest of the world had to heed, had shown up determined to get her money's worth. I suspected she wanted an opportunity to see the burned-out village and pick up some tasty tidbits for her next Thursday morning kaffee klatsch.

I walked her down the carpeted corridor to the front door and saw her out with a little reassuring small talk.

But I'm sure the professional smile on my face dimmed a little as I saw Ben just coming up the pathway. Maria's radar had easily spotted the good-looking man, and she wasn't able to resist stopping and putting a consoling hand on his arm. She murmured a few words which, fortunately, I couldn't hear. But from the bemused and slightly fearful expression on his face, I guessed she'd said something seductive.

I smothered a grin and tried to keep the professional look going as he reached the door where I was standing, and with a haunted glance backwards, he said, "That older lady... Is she one of your clients?"

"Mrs. LeBlanc? Yes, she is. A charming elderly lady."

Ben's expression was priceless. "She, er, just told me that if you didn't know a good thing when you saw it, she'd be very appreciative if I dropped over to her place...and brought my handcuffs."

That did it—I burst out laughing so hard I had to grasp the door frame for support.

Ben's look soured. "It might be funny to you—you deal with these weirdos all the time. But...but...she gave me her card with her address on it..."

"Don't worry, honey—she's pretty harmless. At least, that's my diagnosis."

"That's a relief."

"Yes, I'd say you're about thirty years too old for her taste."

Call me vindictive, but I got a lot of satisfaction from Ben's panicked expression at that moment.

Who'd have thought my big bad cop ex could be scared of a little old lady?

****

I keep referring to Ben as my ex, which isn't strictly true. We did break up after our daughter Becky's disappearance. The turmoil of that would be enough to break even the strongest relationship, but we had professional differences, too.

For example, Ben believed the bad guys were bad, if not evil, and in locking up the bad guys and throwing away the key, which was pretty much incompatible with my psychologist's belief that most human bad behavior was the result of either poor nurturing, character flaws, traumatic experience, or chemical imbalance, and could for the most part be cured.

In short, I didn't believe in evil. Ben did, but then he'd seen a lot more of it than I had.

So then he sent me divorce papers, which was a bit of a shocker for some reason. I signed them and sent them right back. Then I had got caught up in a murder and, with my own life on the line, Ben had ridden in to rescue me from a particularly unsavory ending.

After that, the idiot never got around to signing the divorce papers he'd initiated. Odd behavior for a rational guy, wouldn't you say?

"So is it safe to come in? No crazies lurking in your office, no oddballs in the kitchen? No sex-mad pensioners lying in wait?"

"I resent that, I really do. We're only staying here until we can get settled elsewhere, because we need to be here for work and for the school bus and everything," Sandy McDonagh said plaintively from where she was sitting with her family at my kitchen table, enjoying a late brunch.

"Besides, Dr. Pelham invited us to stay as long as we wanted," Jacko, her son, added. "I've a couple of friends coming over to listen to music later. I hope that's okay."

Gulp! Of course, if I said it wasn't okay, I'd look like a mean monster...and the kid knew it.

Like I said, it's like union station in my house sometimes.

"I'm sorry, Mrs. er...McDonagh, isn't it? I didn't know there was anyone other than Gracie at home. I certainly wouldn't question your right to be here. I know you're Gracie's guests."

Sandy burst out laughing. "It's okay, dear—I was just joshing you. Anyway, we're just about done here. The boys need to get to school, and I'd better show up and start serving the starving masses their donuts and coffees."

Sandy pulled on her woolen jacket and the boys grabbed their bookbags and gym bags and they were gone.

I took a deep breath and went over to the coffee maker to pour two large mugs of the elixir. I had this definite feeling that I was about to hear something I really didn't want to know.

"We need to talk, Gracie—in private." Ben's face was closed, serious, and I felt a funny little shiver go up my spine. Nodding, I handed him one of the mugs and led him into my office, with its muted lighting through rice-paper blinds and its calming color scheme. Ben looked around appreciatively before seating himself in one of the deep leather armchairs where clients were comfortable enough to tell me their troubles.

Would Ben? I wondered.

Turned out it was more like *my* troubles he was telling me about.

"As you can imagine, much of the victim`s clothing was damaged in the fire. But we did find just one small piece of paper saved in his shirt pocket. And, it seems, a similar piece of paper was found at the other murder scenes, too."

"Oh." What else could I say?

"Aren`t you curious, Gracie?"

I chewed on my bottom lip, a sure sign of the creeping sense of anxiety that was overtaking me. "Maybe you could stop beating around the bush and being dramatic," I snapped. "What do you want to tell me?"

Ben reached into the breast pocket of his expensively tailored suit—he always did choose clothes that suited him—and pulled out a plastic zippy bag.

Placing it flat on the desk, he pushed the bag towards me. "Didn't you tell me you had no knowledge of Ralph Morris?"

There was a small oblong of cardboard nestled in the plastic. I didn't want to look, some kind of native foreboding dominating my otherwise logical thoughts, but my eyes were inexorably drawn to the small piece of paper. It was blackened, no doubt from soot during the fire—and my stomach clenched as I remembered it came from the body of a young man who'd died not fifty feet from my home. He probably died while I lounged in my bed, glass of wine in one hand and a detective novel in the other... The paper tugged my eyes back, and there was no mistaking this was a business card.

My business card. A discreetly worded grey-blue oblong with my name, contact phone numbers, and email address. Nothing else to identify my profession, so only the person who had received the card would be aware of its purpose. My card was designed so that no one else would be privy to the shameful secret that the cardholder was seeing or planning to see someone. A therapist. A psychologist.

"This could have come from anywhere—I keep them in my bag, my car, my jacket pocket, hand them out to lots of people, including complete strangers—I could easily have dropped one."

"It's interesting that you didn't wonder if this young man was a client of yours," Ben said mildly.

"Why would I? Don't you think I would remember his name? Ralph Morris?"

"So you can't think of any reason why he had your card in his shirt breast pocket?"

I stared at Ben, alternating between a sick guilt and a hot anger. *Just what was he implying?*

"The only way he could have my card is to have gotten it from someone else who had one, a relative or friend... Perhaps someone recommended me. Another client. Or he might have found it on the street, or maybe he went through my car or my trash. I have no idea!" I struggled to keep the anxiety out of my voice.

Ben was silent for a while. "He could have got it from his killer," he finally said, pinning me to my chair with his dark gaze. Heat raged through me, and then cold. I shivered in my cozy office as I thought about that possibility.

"I hope you don't think I killed him?" I managed to croak, half-jokingly, needing to break the silence. I looked at the smooth desk surface, the small voice-activated tape recorder and pile of tapes filled with clients' ramblings about their worries and thoughts. I gazed out between the partially raised blinds at the windows to the fading day beyond. Anything but look at Ben and see that he wasn't smiling.

"I don't think you killed this man, Gracie. But I'm not the only officer involved, and there are questions. Consider this—you're privy to a lot of secrets, and those secrets may have upset someone. You also work with some hard cases and unsavory types. Maybe you upset someone like that, and he came around here—it wouldn't take a rocket scientist's brain to find out your address. Perhaps he wanted to frighten you, to shut you up. Maybe you even found him breaking into your home during the fire when everyone was distracted. He was trying to steal your files, and you walked in on him.

"Perhaps you fought with him, maybe you were afraid he'd harm you and you grabbed a knife, stabbing him. And then you panicked when you realized he was dead. You used the cover of darkness and the chaos of the fire to drag the body away from your home, hide it and hope that the fire would destroy him and any evidence that tied him to you. He was a slightly built kid. Or maybe your supervisor helped you…"

I wanted to laugh because the scenario was so far from my quiet, routine life. Then I wanted to slap Ben hard and make him take back the words. "I can't believe you could even postulate such a thing," I murmured when I could speak again.

"Like I said, Gracie, I'm not the only officer involved in this case. Some of the guys see this as a reasonable scenario."

"Get out of my house! Get out!" I jumped to my feet, shouting, my heart pounding so hard I thought it would fly out of my chest.

Ben sighed, his face pale. Then he got up and

walked out of the room. Moments later I heard the front door slam behind him, and then I let out the breath I'd been holding.

I'd been an avid member of our local theatre group, but this was one role I had never seen myself in. That of a murderer.

Chapter Five

"Mommy! Mommy!"

With a jolt, I sat up in bed and rubbed my bleary eyes to clear them of sleep. Then I tensed: Becky! Becky was calling for me! She'd had a nightmare...

Panicked, I threw back the covers, swung my feet to the chilly wooden floor, and ran towards the door of her bedroom...

And came awake with a shock from what I knew must have been a dream. I was standing in the echoing emptiness of the small box room that had been my bedroom, once upon a time when I'd stayed with Grannie during the long summers of my childhood. Once there'd been a kid-sized bed and a chest of drawers, a colorful quilt that Grannie and her sisters had worked on during winter nights by the fire. The room had been my sanctuary from the reality of my parents; their messy divorce, and the other hurts that had ravaged my childhood.

Becky had only stayed here once, when we visited Grannie shortly before the stroke that took her to what she had often described as "a better place," but my daughter had loved the little room, too.

Now it was as empty as my arms. My child was gone. Becky had been missing almost five years, years that seemed like an eternity.

I might never see her again. Was my Becky in "a

better place" too? The thought was like a knife to my heart.

Alone in the gloomy moonlight, I sank to the hardwood floors and wept, my arms wrapped around my knees like a child.

****

"Is everything all right, Gracie? I thought I heard you moving about in the night," Sandy McDonagh asked as she swiped butter over a piece of toast at my kitchen table the next morning. "I thought you sounded upset."

I turned to the coffee maker to pour myself a fresh cup, hoping she wouldn't see the blush that stained my face or notice my swollen eyelids. I was embarrassed at my reaction to the dream—and disconcerted at the subject matter. The dream had been so vivid that it had taken me minutes after I woke to realize where I was. I was in the tiny bedroom with its mural of kittens and puppies playing in a flower garden, and I knew with a sharp sense of pain that it really was a dream. It had been a couple of years since I'd dreamed like this in the bitter aftermath of Becky's disappearance.

"Oh, I just remembered that I needed some documents from one of the boxes in the spare room," I mumbled in answer to Sandy's question, adding a silent prayer of thanks that my nocturnal wanderings hadn't taken me into one of the bedrooms that the McDonagh family were camped out in. *Wouldn't that have been cause for some village discussion!*

"And you needed to look at two a.m.?" Sandy said, her eyebrows raised, as I sat down opposite her at the table. This was a blessedly quiet early morning time, the two McDonagh boys off on the school bus and Mac McDonagh gone to work. I'd hoped to savor it, not be cross-examined by my houseguest.

"I doubt I'm the only one finding it hard to sleep after everything that's happened," I said shortly.

Sandy immediately looked contrite. "Oh, Gracie, I'm sorry—I'm not being very sensitive, am I? I know you had to contend with finding that poor boy's body as well as the fire. No wonder you couldn't settle."

She put her hand on my arm briefly, a touch of comfort, and I was instantly sorry for snapping at her. "We've all been through so much—you've lost your home and you probably lost so much of your stuff, too."

"Well, at least we got out alive, and no one was hurt, thank goodness. Billy's still heartbroken about losing Sally, but we're still hoping she'll come out when she's not so frightened."

"Sally?" I didn't know there was another in the McDonagh brood.

"Sally is Jacko's pet rat. She's grey, for all the world like a common barn rat, but she's the cutest little girl you could wish to meet. She's so affectionate, and she likes to sleep in the boys' laundry basket."

"That must make doing laundry quite an adventure for you!"

Sandy grinned, which lit up her face and turned her from pretty to, well, quite lovely. "I must admit I'm not big on rats around the house, and especially in the laundry basket. But this one, she's such a pet. Although the first time I accidentally picked her up in a pair of Jacko's briefs, well, you probably heard my screams up here."

By this time, we'd reached a space for companionable silence, and moments ticked by as we finished up the toast and coffee. Sandy got up, brushing crumbs from the front of her sweater onto the table, and began to clear away her plate and cup.

"I should be off to work—the boss says to take a day or two, but I know I'm going to need time off next week when we move into our new place, so I'm holding off for that."

"You've found a place, then? Already?"

Sandy grimaced. "We're moving into an apartment, one of the triplex buildings down on Oak Tree Road. It's not my first choice, but it keeps us in Jacques Station, and it'll do for the time being. We'll see if the landlord is going to rebuild the house, or if something else comes up. I'd love to buy a place of our own, but we don't have a down payment and the bank won't look at us for a mortgage because we had a rough time with our credit record when Mac was unemployed last winter."

"You know you can stay here as long as you want, if you'd rather wait for something else to come up."

"Thank you—you've been good to us, Gracie, and I don't know what we'd have done if we'd had to take the temporary accommodation they were offering in Kingston. Mac would have lost his job, for sure, because of the travel time. And the boys' school would have been disrupted—they'd have had to go to a new school in the city, mid-term. I appreciate that you gave us the time to get our feet back under us and wait for something local to come up. It's made the world of difference."

"I'm glad. We've all lost something in this fire."

"You know what I miss the most? The boys' baby pictures. I had little locks of their hair, too, in envelopes, and the first baby teeth they lost—sounds a bit ghoulish, doesn't it?"

"Not at all," I said, remembering that I had the same

souvenirs of Becky, tucked away in an album upstairs. Not that there was a lot—Becky was only five when she disappeared.

"Well, better be off to serve coffee and doughnuts to the starving masses again," Sandy said, pulling her coat off the hook by the front door. She worked at a popular doughnut shop in the next town over, and I knew she really enjoyed the job. She said she met the nicest people, and her boss was a great guy. I was glad they were able to stay in Jacques Station, and that they would be able to rebuild their lives here rather than having to decamp into a busy city and find new jobs and new schools That much change in their lives, especially for the boys, would have left its mark, and losing their home and treasured belongings was bad enough.

With a sigh, I picked up the breakfast dishes and began loading the dishwasher. Through my kitchen window I could see the street bathed in sunlight, yet the light only seemed to throw into terrible relief the burned and shattered buildings that embroidered each side of the road.

I was sure I wasn't the only one who would measure life as BTF and ATF—Before The Fire, and After The Fire.

****

The melancholy mood continued. It was Wednesday, after all.

I've come to think of my Wednesday afternoons as The Heartbreak Hour.

I'd meet with eight women in a drab church hall, each pouring grief and pain into the air, sad, angry, tearful, filled with a sorrow that can know no resolution because it derives from so senseless a cause, and because it can never be remedied.

These are women badly hurt by the loss of a son or daughter to drugs. Women who attend the weekly session, women who crave justice. But justice requires that the damage be repaired, and the lives of the victims restored to what they were before.

For these women, life can never return to what it was. Their dead sons and daughters can never be returned to them, so justice can never be done. And because there are so many questions, closure can never ease their pain.

And so, every Wednesday, we meet in the church basement, chosen for its anonymity in these rural townships, and the women talk and listen, cry some, scream some, support and comfort each other. And then each goes away to face her lonely heartbreak again. Because, while for me this is Heartbreak Hour, for these women it's a life sentence.

I'm a counseling psychologist, and each Wednesday I donate a few hours of my time to leading the therapy group for women who have lost a child to drug abuse. The women are from all walks of life, all ages, different backgrounds and beliefs. We meet in the church basement because, unlike my office, they can come here without anyone guessing why. It's hard enough for them to discuss their grief and suffering with each other, without having to explain to neighbors in this rural community why they're seeing a shrink.

For some of them, it's an overdose that robbed them of their child. For others, an accident or act of violence that occurred during a drug-incensed event. One son died in jail, serving time for dealing to pay for his own habit. Another woman's daughter suffocated in her own vomit after friends dared her to take ecstasy along with the alcohol she was too young to be drinking.

My specialty is forensic psychology—the understanding of abnormal or criminal psychology, now so popular in crime fiction—but most of my work is in counseling. I live in God's Country—rural Ontario—and I found out quickly that there plenty of clients to work with, depressed clients, phobias, relationship difficulties, all the way from cabin crazy to deranged…and every shade between.

Most of my clients are just ordinary folk needing a little help getting over grief or some other trauma, dealing with the problems of everyday life. Then there are the ex-cons, the sex offenders and pedophiles I meet with weekly in the safety of halfway house settings.

Except for my Wednesday group, a ragtag band of women from different walks of life and backgrounds, all bound together by one awful sorrow, meeting in a quaint church hall to discuss, rehash, and sometimes, I think, to polish and preserve the pain of their loss.

I'm group leader, moderating, coaxing, questioning, reflecting their words back at them in hopes they'll find their way through the dark maze and into the light. While I've never lost anyone like this, I do know about grief and loss. And I'm trained to help, to gently ease the sharp tang of grief, trained to spot the ones who are in real trouble. The ones who are in danger of following their loved ones into the grave.

But with the Heartbreak Hour, my training let us all down. Because, while I could spot suicidal tendencies, nothing in my knowledge and experience prepared me for what happened.

****

The whole ambience of the group had changed two weeks ago, when we had a new client join in, a thirty-something woman I could tell at a glance was going to be trouble. For one thing, before the arrival of Sophia Scott, the group had settled into their own routine, and an even number meant they could 'partner' each other if we did some of the distracting exercises that sometimes help at awkward moments in a therapy group. Now the number was unbalanced—someone would be without a partner.

But more than that, where the other women expressed a myriad of grief-related emotions, Sophia Scott was always angry. Angry and mean. She'd decry statements of reconciliation from the other women, urge them to join in her anger, aiming it like a scattergun at everyone—the police, the drug dealers, women whose children were still alive, the courts, society in general—and me in particular. She seemed to reserve the worst of her venom for me, possibly because she saw me as an authority symbol, perhaps because, as she claimed, I was trying to get the women to forget their anger over their dead children. Trying to get them to move on and let the people who'd allowed this to happen, who'd turned their backs on the drugged kids, let them get away with their negligence and discrimination.

At first the other women had defended me, insisted I was helping them, that I didn't ignore their pain and anger, didn't urge them to forget that the world had no concern over a dead drug-addicted teen.

But I noticed that this had slowly changed. There was an increased moroseness in the attitudes of some of the others, they came in late, they talked when I was talking, ignored or were rude to some of their fellow group members.

And I had the feeling that things were going to come to a head today—and that Sophia Scott was going to be right in the epicenter of things.

Everyone was present when I walked into the basement, and I wondered if perhaps my foreboding had been wrong. The chairs had been set out in a circle; the women were sitting quietly.

But the cheerful "good day, everyone" I started to utter died on my lips. Three women were sitting in a cluster with Sophia, tight-lipped with rage. Tiny Julia Scannell, a middle-aged country woman who would hardly say boo to a goose, was sitting at a distance from the others, sobbing quietly into a huge white embroidered handkerchief, while the other two women present sat staring down at their feet in obvious discomfort.

I took a deep breath, trying to look unconcerned as I plumped up the back support cushion that I carry with me to ease the aches and pains of sitting at attention for an hour at a time.

Finally, I sat down and looked at each of the women in turn. "What's going on?"

Silence, aside from Julia's muffled sniffling.

I waited them out, looking at each in turn. Finally, Vera Lancer spoke, without looking me in the eye.

'What do you mean?" She was one of the women sitting next to Sophia, and her voice had an edge to it I had not heard before.

"Well…usually, you all make a great effort to say hello when we get together for the group, you show a lot of concern and interest in what each of you has been doing and you're very supportive of each other. Or most of you are." I lanced a knowing look at Sophia and saw her grin.

I could feel my blood heating as I realized what had been going on. But this was a therapy group—far be it from me to tell them what they should be doing.

"I noticed when I came in that the people on this side of the room," indicating Sophia and cronies, "look angry and tight-lipped. Except for Sophia, who looks…I don't know—how would you say you look, Sophia?"

"I don't know what you mean, Dr. Pelham—I'm actually quite upset."

"Ah, you're upset. And Julia there is in tears. Does that mean you are both upset together? Or upset with each other?"

"Stupid fat bitch—spouting off about the Bible, she was. I told her that it wasn't her god that killed my Stevie, it were a sodding druggie. But that her god had sat there and been all…"

"All I said was that vengeance is the Lord's. That we need to move past the anger and learn to remember the good things about our children…" Julie raised her head and looked at me for support.

"Okay, two things. First off, Sophia, we don't swear, curse, or make nasty comments about another member of the group. This is a group to support mothers who are going through what is probably one of the worst things that can happen—the death of a child."

"Yeah, go on, make it all my fault."

"Just let me finish. Julia, it's also part of our agreement that we won't try to push our religious beliefs onto someone else. I know you find your faith a great comfort, but Sophia may need to deal with her sorrow in another way."

"She's evil, that's what she is."

My eyes must have gone wide, because Julia angry like this was a shock.

The other women started to chime in, and I was looking into the faces of a therapy group gone mad. Before I could formulate a way to pull things back to their usual calm, reassuring atmosphere, Rainey Briggs, one of the women sitting next to Julia, said, "It's her fault, Dr. Gracie. That Sophia was a real cow to Julia—she's there telling us all we should get mad and get even, and when Julia said that God was the one who'd punish whoever dragged our kids into drugs, Sophia went off the deep end."

At that point, Sophia launched herself across the small space and tried to sock Rainey in the face. Fortunately, I'm a veteran of highly emotionally charged situations and I got in between the two women—taking a hard punch to the shoulder from Sophie's fist for my troubles.

The violence seemed to shock the other women into action, and they gathered around, grabbing Sophia and Rainey, keeping them apart, while one of them, Janey Barnes, put her arm around me and helped me back to my seat.

I gulped around the pain that was still shooting down my arm—there would be a big enough bruise on my shoulder by night—and said in a very quiet but authoritative voice, 'Sit down, all of you. I'm shocked that it has come to this."

"Yeah, Dr. Fancy Pants Pelham—you like everything to be nicey-nice, don't ya? Don't want to rock the boat at all, just sweep everything under the rug and let's pretend it's all okay. You don't give a shit, really, about our kids being dead," Sophia taunted.

"Sophia, I think you have way too much anger for this group to be able to help you. At least, not yet. I'm going to suggest that you leave the group, for the time being, and that you come and see me for some private counseling. Let's see if we can…"

"Go to hell! You're throwing me out of the group because you can't bear being shown up for the big coverup you're doing. You're just trying to keep the lid on, and if you think I'm going to sit around with you and pay…"

"I wasn't going to ask you to pay, Sophia. This group is free, and any extra counseling that anyone in the group needs, I do pro bono…"

"Pro what? Keep your fancy words and your nicey-nice attitudes, you condescending cow. I'll tell you one thing—rather than being all understanding and everything, all those yobbos who deal drugs to our kids should be strung up."

Sophia got up and walked out. The three women sitting with her looked at each other and then they, too, got up and walked towards the door. One of them. Elsie Babinau, turned around at the door, her face red.

"I'm sorry, Dr. Gracie. I know you've done your best. But it's just not working for me anyway. Sophia has made me see that."

"Well, all of you—you know that you are welcome to return to group any time you wish," I told their departing backs.

Now there were just four of us in the room—back to an even number again. But I couldn't help thinking I'd missed something, not picked up on something that these women needed from me, that I'd let them all down.

The thought stayed with me the rest of the day, and I was depressed as hell when I got back home.

****

Finding Ben just getting out of his car as I arrived home actually lightened my mood. His tall, unflappable presence always seemed to reach out to me. We'd been so good together—what a pity we couldn't get over the high walls that we'd built round ourselves individually to try to cope with the deep grief over the loss of our baby girl. Perhaps if we could have grieved together, it would have been different.

I wanted to go into his arms, have him hold me the way he'd always done, to feel protected and safe. Ben always said that it was very flattering to him to have an independent, educated lady like me seek protection in his arms.

Seeing him now, I hungered in a way that nothing could quench.

But the walls were too high.

Chapter Six

I was deeply asleep when the sound woke me up. At first, I thought it was just an owl or some other night creature, cats fighting in the rubble, perhaps—God knows, Jacques Station seems to be drop-off central for every unwanted cat and kitten in Ontario. To say nothing of the rednecks who somehow think it's a smear on their manhood—or femininity—to have their pets neutered.

I turned over and pulled the covers up to my ears, yawned and prepared to go back to sleep. Then I heard it again. I sat up, swallowing hard as my mind screamed, "No!" and my heart screamed, "Yes!" The sound came again.

"Mommeeee!"

I was out of bed and running down the stairs in my bare feet before I'd even had time to process what I was hearing. Throwing open the kitchen door, I ran into the garden and there she was. Sitting on the old wooden rope swing that I'd played on as a kid during the long-ago summers with Grannie.

My long-lost daughter, Becky. She was calling my name, and when she saw me, she held out her chubby baby arms and smiled that radiant smile... "Mommy, bring me home..."

And then she was crying, the sort of crying that tears at her mother's heart.

I couldn't bear to hear my baby cry like that.

And that's when sanity prevailed, and I woke up, still tucked up in my warm bed, but I was shivering…

Because my Becky was no longer a baby. She'd be ten now, her chubby baby arms and golden ringlets would have given way to the beginnings of an adolescent figure and probably a modern hairstyle. The baby on the swing was all in my imagination, born of longings that I thought I'd tucked away and filed under "impossible dreams."

So why had the dreams of my kidnapped daughter suddenly surfaced now?

****

"I think you know why, without my analyzing it for you," Jack Lennon said later that day as I told him about the dreams of my child. He was avoiding my eyes as he fiddled with a tiny crystal ornament on the table near his chair. We were sitting in the conversation area of Jack's office on my regular debriefing visit. Jack knew about my past, about the disappearance of my only child and the slow disintegration of my relationship with Ben as we both struggled to understand and come to terms with the fact that we'd failed to protect the most precious thing in our lives.

"It's not uncommon for a new trauma to spark memories of an old one. Because of the stress and shock of the fire at Jacques Station, my subconscious has dredged up the memories of my daughter and my own need for closure."

Jack nodded, compassion naked on his face. "You haven't been able to find closure on Becky's disappearance. God knows, it's not surprising that you'd think of her when another awful thing happens in your life."

Unable to look him in the eyes, my gaze was drawn to the mesmerizing turn, turn, turn of the little crystal figure in Jack's stubby pale fingers. It was a figurine, the sort of thing sold in gift stores for people who collected these dust-attracting little items. I'd never been big on that myself. Why bother with something that added to housekeeping chores, something I'd never been that keen on?

We chatted for a few minutes more, desultory on my part, earnest on Jack's, and finally I rose to leave. "Thank you, my friend—you certainly helped me sort out the reason for my dreams and put them into context." I pulled on my quilted jacket and slipped my feet into the boots I had left by the door.

"You know my door is always open to you, Gracie. I hope I have been able to help you through this difficult time. The fire in Jacques Station must have been a terrible trauma for all the residents there. Please don't hesitate to pick up the phone and call me if you need me."

Jack's phraseology made me uncomfortable, not for the first time. As my supervising psychologist, he was supposed to keep our relationship on a purely businesslike, arm's-length level, yet I was finding that it was becoming less acceptable to have such increasingly personal-seeming warmth. I knew that someday I was going to have to do something about his attitude, but I had grown to consider him a friend as well as a colleague, and heaven knows, friends who could understand the work I did as a counselor were few and far between. Because of this I valued Jack's friendship enough to try to keep it formal and from becoming more than friends, even though I was becoming more and more uncomfortable with his attitude. What I needed was a colleague who could understand the trials and tribulations of working with people in need of counseling help. I was worried Jack was stepping outside that boundary.

So it was with mixed feelings I left his pretty little house in a nearby town, and I realized with dismay that I had been so engrossed in my own difficulties that I had not brought up my concerns about the behavior of some of the women in my Wednesday group. I almost turned to go back inside, but the sense that I might be leaning too heavily on Jack at the moment stopped me.

****

I made up my mind to put my worries about the possible suicide of a parolee at the halfway house and the bitter anger infecting my Wednesday group meeting out of my mind. I was sure that, piece by piece, I would be able to handle the irritating and provoking behavior of Seth Marshall in the halfway house group, but the bitter anger of the women who were grieving lost children would be another, more delicate, issue.

On top of everything, I was anxious about the murder of the young man whose body I had found so close to my home. The idea that he had died a violent death while I'd been sleeping peacefully in my bed or going about my evening rituals—watching a favorite TV program, eating a snack, tidying my home—was a heavy weight that left a depression I couldn't describe or shake.

What I needed was a good brisk walk and some company, so I texted Allie and asked if she'd like to take an afternoon stroll around the village with Josh and me. In the silence that followed, I realized what Allie was thinking, and quickly explained that Josh, far from being a new man in my life, was my next-door neighbor's pooch.

Later, when we met up outside the manse, I explained, "I'm walking him while his owner recovers from a broken ankle." I tried hard to keep the amusement out of my tone.

Allie laughed and said she had thought I had a new boyfriend I'd been keeping a secret. "Mind you," she added, "I think having a man in your life would do you the world of good."

I blew her a loud raspberry and we both collapsed in laughter, clinging to each other as the tensions of the day drained away.

Then we were walking along Front Street, where the devastation of the fire was less obvious. Tall hedges of nicely trimmed willow and a flowering shrub I couldn't name seemed to conceal some of the damage to the homes here. It was mainly smoke damage, although the Waltons' property, at the end of the row, was going to need a new roof.

"I think I have enough man trouble in my life, between my supervisor and the miserable collection of misfits in the halfway house program. Then there's my ex, Ben, who seems to pop up like a bad penny every time I think he's forgotten me. Did I tell you he's in charge of the murder investigation?"

Allie couldn't hide her grin. "Maybe, just maybe, he has suddenly realized what he's lost in leaving you, and wants back into your life?"

"Sorry, Allie, I know you're a romantic, but the last time he visited me, he just about accused me of being the murderer of not one but three young men."

We stopped for a moment to let Josh deliver his peemails in the shelter of a tall hedge of lilac trees, the bare branches little protection from the bitter wind.

Allie frowned. "That's not exactly the kind of reconnecting I was imagining," she said, giving me a hug. "And you say three murders? I thought…I thought the young man in the feed store was the one and only…?"

I suddenly realized I'd been talking about information Ben had asked me to keep quiet about. I explained that to Allie and asked her not to mention it to anyone.

"I'm a minister, Gracie. We're used to keeping secrets. But I'll say a prayer for those poor lost souls, and for the police to solve this case before anything else happens."

I knew I could trust my friend. The person I worried about was her horrible lover, Tina. Tina would do anything to get me into trouble. But I couldn't say as much to Allie, who was very defensive about her choice of partner.

Anyway, we were almost back at Allie's church, so we said our goodbyes and I delivered Josh off to his grateful owner and went into my office to draw up plans for the Wednesday meeting. I offered a fervent prayer that by then the women would be back to their gentle selves and the horrible Sophia would have been dethroned.

Chapter Seven

My prayers weren't answered.

Instead, the meeting of the women's group that Wednesday morning was an absolute horror. I was about ready to book a passage to some remote island far, far away from all this craziness.

First of all, two of the mild-mannered, gentle women, Elsie Babinau and Vera Lancer, didn't show up. When I asked if anyone had heard from them, there was a slight, embarrassed silence.

Then Rainey Briggs spoke up in such a quiet voice I had to ask her to repeat what she said.

"They're finding it too confrontational, Gracie. I drove Vera home and she cried the whole way. Neither of them will be coming back until things get better here."

"What do you mean by getting better?" I asked, although I already knew.

"The nastiness and the fighting, the viciousness of that cow over there."

I should have known better than to ask, because Rainey is one of those deep, thoughtful people who don't pull their punches when they finally speak.

"They're a bunch of soft little cowards who don't have courage to stand up and protect their children—and punish anyone who hurts them." Sophia all but growled as she spit out her hate-filled comment.

Well, I guess Sophia had put her cards on the table.

"What would you have them do, Sophia? They can't bring their children back to life, and I don't think nastiness is helping any."

Sophia and the little group around her were smirking.

Sophia stood up and her squad, now reduced to two, stood. "We believe that sitting around doing nothing is, well, doing nothing. There're other kids out there who're vulnerable. We intend to protect them."

"And how would you protect them?" I asked.

"Me, I believe in get mad and get even. The drug-dealing slime should be made to pay."

And with that chilling statement, Sophia and her crew walked out, slamming the heavy room door behind them.

The silence left behind was deafening. Finally, Elsie spoke up. "I can't be doing with this, Gracie. We're here to try and find some peace in the loss of our babies, and yet it feels like we're in the middle of a war. All that Sophia and her buddies seem to want is violence. Like I said, I can't be doing with this."

And Elsie got up and gathered her purse and jacket. Then one by one, Janey, Julia, and Rainey and the others stood and did likewise.

"We're so sorry, Gracie. We know you mean well, but, well, this is not helping."

And I was left alone in the echoing church hall to wallow in my failure.

****

By some nasty quirk of Fate, Mr. John Haggarty, the supervisor in charge at the halfway house, called and said they had some event or another going on and he wondered if I could change my planned Thursday meeting to Wednesday evening.

The group at the halfway house consists of men convicted to various levels of pedophilia. That's one of the many reasons Ben claims my working with these people when they have just been released from prison is disgusting.

Good heavens, how I wanted to say, *No! No! Not after the nightmare that had been that morning's women's group.*

But in the back of my mind, I remembered Lyle Richmond, the shy little man who had left me worried at the last meeting. I think Lyle could well be considering an attempt at suicide. Strictly speaking, to my mind, I really didn't think he should be classed with the hardcore kiddie rapists.

No, he was caught with a couple of hundred pics of little kids in various poses. That would be enough to cause apoplexy in many less experienced people, and there was always the long-standing question of what happened to those children. Was it just a fun game to them to mug in front of the camera?

Or, as many people thought, was it just a prelude to skin on skin or worse with a real, live child?

I admit I felt the need for a quiet nap after the women's group disaster, but after that I could hardly summon up enough enthusiasm to drag myself out in time for the late afternoon session at the halfway house.

****

As it happened, I managed to put on a reasonable performance of listening, consoling, and occasional advising that makes up a counselling session.

The real aim is to get the participants to talk, to reveal their worries, anxieties, and, in some cases, the dark side of their desires. The idea being to discover the origins of their behavior and carefully try to change their needs and desires.

Or, as someone said, to at least put the fear of the Almighty in them to be sure they keep their dirty paws to themselves.

You have to swallow down your repulsion, sometimes, as these men describe the behaviors that give them joy, behaviors with innocent young children and with teens, that most of us find repugnant, even cruel in the damage it can cause.

I always advise anyone who reveals—or who appears to perhaps have been a victim of these abusive behaviors—to seek some form of counselling. It may include bringing in police and taking legal action against the perp, but in the long run for most victims, being open actually helps in the healing process. Keeping such pain, anger, and confusion buried deep inside can only eat away at a person's sense of self.

But enough of that. My work with the men in the halfway house, convicted child abusers and rapists, is intended to make them see the error of their ways, to learn how to contain their impulses, and to stop any further activities.

A tall order, especially when you're dealing with men who have mixed feelings about whether they want to stop or not, or even may still believe that what they do to their young victims is "love." The prospect of going back to do jail time might be a pretty strong incentive to stay away from kids, but for all too many, the incentive just isn't enough. Not when they can tell themselves they're doing no harm, they really love those kids.

Of course, I do have a secret reason of my own for

working with these men—who sometimes turn my stomach with their declarations of illicit love, or that they're doing nothing wrong, or even worse, their descriptions of that they have done.

You see, I am still searching for my beautiful daughter, who I dropped off at an innocent-looking child's birthday party with her friends—and was never seen again.

I don't know if I dread the idea that she fell victim to one of these men, or whether I would prefer that someday her little body is found, perhaps having fallen into a stream or a crag in the woods. But my greatest wish—one I never speak out loud—is that Becky will be found alive and well. Maybe she was taken in by another family, perhaps taken across the border and left there to be brought into the social services process and adopted by a nice family.

I cry when I imagine this. Even five years later, I think my heart will break all over again.

Sometimes I think I see a child who could be Becky, and more than once I have made a fool of myself by approaching such a little girl now almost eleven years old and being chastised by the mother.

One time I even had an angry father threaten to call the police on me, until I explained the mistake and apologized tearfully.

Which brings me back to the reasons I work with men convicted of child molestation and worse.

I keep alive a hope that, one day, one of them will tell me they have seen Becky. Or they know what happened to her. Or where I could find her.

Which leaves me working with men I would otherwise despise, whose idea of small talk turns my stomach. But I cannot stop.

Even though it cost me my marriage.

****

John Haggarty, my boss in charge of the halfway house unit, stopped me as I made my way from the lockers to the room that was used for the counselling sessions. I could tell immediately by the look on his face that this was serious.

"Could we have a word in private, Gracie?" As he closed the door, he added, "Take a seat, Gracie." He bit his upper lip, a tell I'd noticed before when he had something difficult to disclose.

"What is it, John?" I pressed, uncomfortable at his seriousness.

"Only a few days ago you expressed concern about Lyle Richmond. You thought he was extremely depressed, so I had the staff keep as close an eye as possible on him."

My stomach clenched. Of all the cons in the halfway house, I always felt Lyle was the least dangerous. There was something very innocent about him. "Was it a suicide attempt?"

John paused. He took a deep breath and replied, "No, although in a way, it was as good as."

"What did he do?" Tears were pooling in my eyes. "I should have spent some time with him, helped him…"

John shook his head. "You have nothing to blame yourself for, Gracie. It appears Seth Marshall was giving Lyle a hard time, calling him names and so on, telling him he was too weak to have a proper good time with any kid…"

"That bastard! Oh, my god…"

John sighed. "It seems that he goaded Lyle too far,

and the smaller man leapt at Seth, trying to stab him with a pair of scissors—I'm not sure where he got them from. Anyway, he grazed Seth's arm, but Seth took the scissors and… Well, he stabbed Lyle in the chest. Fortunately, the two guys on duty were keeping a close watch, and they stepped in immediately, called an ambulance, patched Seth up…"

"Is Lyle…I mean…"

"Lyle is in the hospital, likely to make a full recovery. Seth has been put in a secure room, where he'll stay until there has been an investigation. It will probably wind up in court, and Seth may be back in prison when it's all over."

I couldn't disguise the anger I felt. "You know, Seth has a good fifty pounds and eight inches on Lyle, hardly a match. And he must have taunted Lyle terribly for him to attack like that."

"Well, we'll have to wait and see what happens with the investigation. It's problematic that Lyle attacked first, with a weapon. That won't play well in the police investigation."

"I'll call by the hospital and speak to Lyle on my way home. Meanwhile, I think it would be a good idea to talk to the other guys and see if there's going to be further problems."

"Are you sure? Things are still a bit… unpredictable—you know how it is when everyone gets filled with adrenalin and nowhere to let it loose—although I did send them to the gym for a while."

I paused. He was offering me a chance to get out from under the fallout from the events, but there was no way I could accept. "Honestly, I think right now it would be better to go ahead with the usual session. The sooner things are got back to whatever passes for normal, the better."

"I knew you'd say something like that, Gracie, but I wanted to give you an out." John smiled, but his expression was tired. He's a man who puts his heart into his work, and when things go wrong, he really feels that he should take the blame.

"So let's get to it. How many of the guys are going to be present today?"

"Well, I think Seth needs a little more time in solitary to think about what happened, and of course, Lyle is otherwise engaged." John gave a wry smile. "So you'll have the rest, unless anyone chooses to cry off. If they do, they have to stay in the building, because I want to be sure we know where everyone is," John explained.

When I walked into the counselling room, I saw immediately that, as well as Seth and Lyle, there were another two missing, apparently opting to stay in the lounge and watch television and read. Which was fine—some quiet down time can help a lot after a traumatic experience.

The ones who remained were very much subdued, but they had questions about what had happened, which I answered to the best of my ability.

When I had finished, there was silence in the room for several minutes, and then Jason Pelligrew spoke up. "I can hardly believe this happened, Miss Gracie. We are men who love children—and, aside from a few exceptions we regard as monsters, if we understand the so-called pedo behavior—but it's awful to think that, in this very room, one of our friends tried to kill another."

"And I'm not sure what Lyle meant to do, although he started it," said Richard.

"You can't blame Lyle, honestly, that Seth never let up on the little guy, since the moment he arrived here he was picking on him," another member of the counselling group, Ray Satchwell, spoke up. I think it was the first time I'd heard that quiet, middle-aged man speak without prompting.

"So, Miss Gracie, what will happen now?"

I thought for a moment about how much I should explain to them. "As you probably know, Seth is being held in a quiet room, and Lyle is in hospital, although his prognosis seems to be good.

"However, the management of the halfway house had to bring the police in, which means there will probably be charges laid. There was no choice in the matter—something this serious has to involve the police."

"Who will be charged? I mean, I know Lyle started it, but it was really Seth's fault."

"Honestly, I can't answer that right now. There is a good chance the police will file charges and both Lyle and Seth will appear in court. This means their probation and time here will be over and one or both of them will face jail terms. Assault of any kind, especially with a weapon, is taken very seriously."

The rest of our time went by in stilted conversation, and I decided, with the group's approval, to end the session a little early. I told them I would visit Lyle in hospital and asked if anyone had anything they wished me to tell him.

After a short silence, Jason, who appeared to have become the group's spokesperson, said, "Can you give Lyle good wishes for a fast recovery from all of us?"

I looked around and saw nods and a general

agreement on the faces of the others, so I agreed I would pass their wishes on to Lyle.

I stopped by the supervisor's office on my way out and told John of the group's reaction to my telling them I would call by the hospital and check on Lyle.

My friend was still shaken and infuriated by what had happened. "How are you feeling, Gracie? This must have shaken you up," he said.

"It could have been a lot worse, I suppose," I told him. "But fortunately, Lyle will recover and maybe Seth will learn that he can't taunt and bully without consequences."

"I admire your optimism." John smiled, and we wished each other goodnight.

At the hospital, I had to sweet-talk one of the nurses into letting me see Lyle, just for a few moments. She pointed out that visiting hours were over, but in the circumstances, she was sure a quick word with Lyle would cheer him up. "His wound is fairly slight but was probably very frightening. He should make a full recovery, but he's very depressed," the nurse told me.

I spent a few minutes with Lyle, passed on the good wishes of the rest of the group—without mentioning Seth—and said I looked forward to seeing him back in the group.

He nodded, but I could tell the drugs he'd been given had blunted his feelings, and he was nodding off to sleep as I quietly slipped from the room.

Chapter Eight

The next morning saw me out and about early after a sleepless night. I figured a good, brisk walk with my doggie friend Josh would maybe blow away the cobwebs of the bad dreams that had disturbed my sleep.

A bonus for being out bright and early was that my friend Allie was also an early riser and her lover, Tina, was a slug-a-bed, not rising until the sun was high in the sky.

Allie caught sight of me through the kitchen window of the manse and I saw her waving furiously. I stopped with the dog, who was happy to spend some time sniffing in the grass along the road and leaving a few peemails of his own.

Allie tiptoed through the heavy manse door, quietly closing it so as not to awaken the sleeping dragon known as Tina. Then she ran lightly down the steps and path to join me on the road. She had slipped a warm jacket on and was still putting on some woolly red gloves as she ran towards me. My friend was a bit out of breath as she joined me at the head of the path towards the Crooked Stream.

"I'm so glad to see you, Gracie! It seems like we don't see anywhere near enough of each other these days. I really enjoyed our walk with you and Josh yesterday," she said, bending to rub the pooch behind his ears and receiving a charming tailwag in return. She paused for a moment to get her breath, her cheeks flushed with the cold.

I was tempted to tell her that we'd see a lot more of each other if it wasn't for her ridiculously jealous and always angry girlfriend, but I decided this was too lovely a day to get into a fight. After all, when it gets to late October, there aren't many more bright and sunny mornings to be enjoyed here in Ontario.

Instead, I hugged her. "Judging from the fat, fluffy clouds gathering above the treeline, it looks like snow is on the horizon, so we have to make the most of an early morning like this."

"Let's walk around the village and see what more changes have been made. There seems to be nonstop work going on, with the big trucks hammering around," Allie said, bending down again to ruffle the fur around Josh's ears. The dog's tail went into swishing overdrive to express his pleasure.

I paused. "I'm not sure I want to see anymore. I'd thought of taking a walk alongside the stream and through the woods instead," I told her.

"I'm feeling pretty frisky this morning, so why don't we see if we can do both, and then we'll stop on my back porch and enjoy a Saturday glass of vino!" Allie had a mischievous glint in her eye.

I laughed. "A glass of wine, early in the morning? Whatever would your congregation say? And more scarily, whatever would your sweetheart, the dragon Tina, have to say about that?"

Allie giggled. "Oh, Tina is more smoke than fire— and guess what? She's heading to Peterborough for a job interview. Yes, even on a Saturday morning. I think it's at a thrift store, but it would be good for her to have a job. She does get bored. Anyway, after that she's visiting a friend over there, staying overnight with her, so you needn't be afraid that she'll suddenly appear and breath fire on you…"

We exchanged a small conspiratorial giggle that brightened my heart. It seemed a long time now that Allie's and my friendship had been overshadowed by Tina's jealousy. I took a deep breath of the crisp, clean air, perfumed by the earthy scent of fallen leaves and the icy water that surged along the creek.

By now we were well onto the woodland path alongside the creek, and we could just about see the roofs of the houses along Simon Street, bordering the woods. Here in the shade of the trees it was actually a little chilly. The trees were beautiful with the last of the autumn gold and red leaves fluttering to the ground, and the stream had a thin strip of ice like lace around the edges.

The overhead branches kept out the sun, and soon the chill got to us, so we decided to cut across the woodlands and back onto the path around the village.

"Oh, my goodness—look at the damage to the Anglican church!" Allie exclaimed.

I could hardly bear to look at the old stone building. Although it hadn't been used as a church for a good ten years, a local contractor had purchased it and was working in his spare time to renovate it.

I remembered him, Bill Yates, telling me he had fallen in love at first sight with the building and planned to turn it into a comfortable home for himself and Lizzie Dale, the young woman he planned to marry at Christmas.

"Bill told me how much he loved those beautiful stained-glass windows and the way they created such glorious rainbow patterns on the inside walls when the sun was shining," I told Allie. "He must be quite heartbroken."

Allie agreed. "He put a lot of work into designing the interior, always with an eye to the effects of the antique stained-glass windows. And now it's all gone, Gracie. The heat of the fire shattered those windows into a million little pieces. It's irretrievable."

The rest of our walk was in silence as we took in the damage that was increasingly showing up in the bright, cold sunlight. I thought I was used to the idea of the way our little village had been devastated by fire, but for some reason, as I walked the familiar streets with my friend Allie, I was taken aback again by the further changes.

There were bulldozers and big trucks in front of several of the badly damaged homes and businesses, and in a couple of places along our walk, the buildings with the worst damage had already been completely demolished. The gaps were a painful reminder not just of the destruction of the fire, but of the changes that were coming our way.

"Our village will be almost unrecognizable," I complained to Allie when we stopped at the manse for coffee. We'd agreed that coffee was a better choice than wine before getting on with the chores of our day.

I'd chosen the early morning time for the visit with Allie because I was pretty sure it was safe to see her without her lover Tina hovering around us like a vulture, sneering at me and trying her best to push us apart.

Call me cowardly, sure, but if you'd ever come up against Tina or her like, you'd want to be sure to avoid the nasty attitude too.

We stopped before going into the manse to stand on the top step and look out over the village. The damage was clearly visible, but I took heart from the renewal work that was already ongoing.

"Oh, Gracie, I can hardly bear to look!" Allie said. "Each time I hear the heavy trucks and the bulldozers, I think of the poor souls who have lived in those houses over the years and now have had to cope with this destruction. You know the history of Jacques Station as well as I—did you see that the Morrison home was a total write-off? Try to avoid the corner, there—they've flattened it. And so many years of our local history are also being flattened…"

I bit my lip. "That house was lived in by six generations of the same family, pretty much early settlers. I hope they managed to rescue some of the old documents and photographs they had on display in the great room."

Allie reassured me, saying, "I've heard from a couple of parishioners that some of the historic items from that and other homes were rescued and are being looked after by the Village Historical Society."

"Well, I guess that's good news. The saddest thing is that too many of our people can't afford to rebuild the homes, or their landlords can't, and so they're having to move away. I understand several families are living in motel accommodation in Kingston, and I don't know if they'll ever be able to come back to Jacques Station."

We sat on antique wicker chairs on the deck at the back of the manse, enjoying hot coffee and some of the delicious cookies Allie was famous for. The sky was already darkening with gathering snow clouds. It seemed a fitting tribute to our mood.

Still, times like this were part of why I loved this little village—the quiet, the simple pleasures of sitting outdoors and watching the slow calendar changes in the sky.

Allie stood after a while. "It's starting to get chilly, Gracie, and we should go inside."

"Winter's on its way," I said with a sad smile as I gathered up my jacket and slipped on my boots. "I should be getting back, though—I've a client just after lunchtime. I wonder what the next few months will bring, because there are certainly going to be some changes here."

And I must confess there were tears on my cheeks as I turned the corner and my house came into view—the house built by my great-grandparents and left to me in my grandmother's will. I loved that house, with the wonderful—and sometimes sad—memories stored within its walls, and I was so grateful it had been spared as the fire monster seared through the village.

Then who should I see, waiting in his car parked alongside mine on the front parking area, but that bad penny, my soon-to-be-ex-husband. *Detective Benjamin Pelham? Oh, my, my day can't get any better… Yes. I am being sarcastic.*

****

"So, just as I was beginning to enjoy my day off, you come along. Do you do this deliberately to annoy me, or is there some other method in your nastiness?"

Ben grinned that grin that always turned my innards to warm mush…and once upon a time had made me like putty in his hands.

But not anymore. I had made a vow that I would remove all traces of Ben from my life. And then he came along with a murder investigation and somehow suggested I was involved in the death of a young drug dealer. I've been struggling to prevent him getting into my head, but every time he turns up at my home, I can feel that pull that has always existed between us.

And I hurry to remind myself that those days are over, our marriage is dead and gone, and I'm much better off without him.

And I can almost hear the Universe laughing as it digests the lies I am telling myself. I reply to the little voice in my head that there is too much pain between us, too much resentment, too many lies and cover-ups and misunderstandings. But that little voice inside my head—or is it my heart?—won't let it go and keeps calling me out on that statement.

Still, he's here, tall and handsome in a dark way, and my only hope is to do the best I can to get rid of him. A plan he quickly demolishes.

All these thoughts buzz at warp speed through my head as we stand there on my doorstep, trying to ignore the cold breeze that has whipped through the nearby trees and scattered the rest of the autumn leaves around the road and sidewalk.

"So are we going to stand here until we turn into ice sculptures, or are you going to open the door? I have things we need to talk about." Ben pointedly looked at the key in my hand.

"I think I've seen more of you in the past couple of weeks than I saw of you in months when we were married. And I have a last-minute client coming to see me in about an hour, so you'll have to make it quick. What gives?"

"Open the damn door and I'll tell you all about it."

92

"Oh, you tempter, you!"

Then I saw the weariness in his face. He looked like a man who hadn't slept for some time, and I knew how dedicated Ben was to his work. As the icy breeze continued to swirl around us, promising that heavy snow wasn't far away, I gave in and opened the door to let us both into my house.

Oh, does that heat greeting us feel good!

I set the coffeemaker to the "strong brew" setting after peeling off my parka, while Ben shrugged out of his winter jacket and slumped down on one of my antique kitchen chairs.

"Don't make yourself too comfortable," I warned him as I handed him a mug of coffee, then turned to the refrigerator to bring out the cream. "Sugar is in the blue bowl on the table."

"You wouldn't happen to have a sandwich or something in there, would you?" Ben asked. "I missed breakfast."

I shook my head. "Judging by the look of you, that's not the only meal you've missed. Whatever are you doing, Ben?"

"Just been too busy, that's all. I'm sorry, it's a bit of a cheek of me to ask you to feed me."

Okay, I relented. I knew how hard he worked, how dedicated to fighting the evil that touched our lives.

"How does bacon and egg on toast sound? I can whip that up in a few minutes." *Then I can get him out quickly* was the unspoken thought behind my words.

At last, a smile lit up his face. "You would have my eternal gratitude."

"Yeah, you said something like that when we stood in front of the priest," I muttered under my breath.

Ben heaved a deep sigh. "Gracie, are we always going to behave like sworn enemies? I mean, we had a good thing going, and neither of us will ever get over the loss of our little Becky...but our lives have to go on."

I slammed a frying pan down on the hot ring and began to layer bacon into sizzling fat.

"I know you think I've moved on, Gracie, but the truth is that every time a crime involving a child comes across my desk, I can feel my heart rev up. I'm wondering whether this is our child, is this Becky, can we finally bring her home. And each time I read the details I find myself muttering a prayer that our baby is still alive. And then there's the truth, that the child in question isn't Becky, and it feels as though my heart will explode in my chest."

I kept my back to him as I cooked, because I couldn't bear to see the look of anguish on his face. The same look that was probably on mine.

"You never said anything about that. You would never talk about Becky. It broke my heart."

Ben got up and came and stood beside me. "The truth is, Gracie, that I felt responsible. I felt I should have protected our little girl, saved her. And to see the way you were suffering, it was a reflection of my suffering, too, but I could not burden you with it. I felt I had to be strong for both of us. Stupidly, that meant never showing you that I, too, was grieving. That I was living in hope that one day...one day we might find our little girl. And I lived in dread of that day, which sounds at odds with what I've just said. But I was afraid that we would find her...and she wouldn't be..."

"Oh, Ben, I know what you're saying. I dream of Becky, dream that she's calling for me, and in my sleep,

I go looking for her…but she's not real. I'm still afraid that one day there'll be a call that our child has been found. And that there's nothing left of her but a broken body…"

I turned towards Ben, and he wrapped me in his arms. I leaned against him, feeling his strength, and his pain that was reflected in my own.

A few moments later he pulled away. "I wish we could have had this conversation years ago. Perhaps there would have been some way of healing, together. Instead of…"

"Instead?"

"Instead, you're burning the bacon…!"

He was right. A few moments longer on the hot ring and the bacon would have been, well, toast.

Despite the seriousness of our conversation, we were both laughing as I cracked eggs into the cooler pan, along with a couple of tomato halves, and popped bread into the toaster.

Finally, I handed Ben a plate piled with bacon and eggs—what my grandmother called "a heart attack on a plate"—and pointed him to the table where I had already put out ketchup and cutlery. I added fresh mugs of coffee for us both, then sat down at the table while Ben ate.

"I take it you've been missing a fair number of meals?" I teased him as he wolfed down the food.

"You know what it's like. No time for meals…"

"And no time for family, either?" I added and was instantly ashamed by the pained look on his face. "I'm sorry. That was a low blow. We should be able to be a bit more civilized after we've been apart for so long."

He nodded, his mouth full.

"So what aren't you telling me, Ben? Why are you

here?"

Ben paused, took a swallow of the fresh coffee, and I knew he was putting his thoughts in order. As a cop, he also had to be careful just how much he said.

"Ralph Morris is the third known young drug dealer to die in the Frontenac County area in the last three weeks. All three were young men—the oldest was twenty-five. All died violently."

"How…how…were they killed? Do you think maybe it's some kind of gang war going on?" I tried to quell the sick feeling in my stomach as I thought of all the grief the loss of these young men would mean to their families.

"It seems all three were stabbed. I can't tell you more than that—we're waiting for the last two autopsies, and then we can compare all three and maybe get a handle on why and who."

And I couldn't get out of my head the idea that a young man had lain so close to my home, dying, and I'd probably been glued to the TV, or working on my laptop, or fast asleep, all unaware of his suffering. But now another thought crept into my mind and chased sleep away for a long time.

Three apparently related deaths meant that a killer with no conscience, a psychopath, might be on the loose in our quiet little neighborhood.

Ben had just left when there was a knock on the door—he was back again, with a grubby white envelope in his hand.

"This was under your car's rear window wiper," he said, handing it to me. "Looks like it may have been there a while."

I took the envelope from him. It felt soggy in my

hand and looked as though it could have been tucked in there when I was at the halfway house in Kingston, and it had travelled back to Jacques Station in that precarious position.

It was quite a feat for the flimsy envelope to have stayed where it was put. It had been pitch dark that night when I arrived home from the not-so-fun outing at the halfway house and the visit with Lyle last night. I was so tired, and I could have had half a dozen kangaroos clinging to the rear window wiper and I'd never have noticed.

I sighed. "It looks like some kind of advertising flyer. They're always being stuck on cars. Guess it's cheap advertising. They're pretty tiresome. They either blow away in the weather or they're thrown into the gutters, adding to the litter mess. It's usually for twenty-five percent off some sandwich bar offerings, or an ad for some concert I don't want to go to," I muttered, tossing the offending piece of paper in the garbage.

Chapter Nine

I was curious when I got a text message from Alicia James, daughter of the man sometimes called the king of Jacques Station because his family had once owned the place, lock, stock, and barrel. They had also owned the railway holdings and goodness knows what else. Their holdings had shrunk a little in past years, but there was no doubt about who owned the town, and almost everything in it.

She said she'd call by my home later to talk to me, so I was left wondering what was happening. That the queen of Jacques Station might be coming to visit me was an idea out of left field, but even so, peasant that I am, I flew around my entryway, tidying up in a bid to maintain the smooth, calm atmosphere I had worked so hard to achieve in my office. It's a place where, at least so I hope, my clients can relax and feel safe.

I even went to empty the garbage can, and that's when I noticed that grubby, water-stained white envelope Ben had found on my car. I was about to throw it out when I noticed it had my name written on it in a childish scrawl. The letters were written in some kind of colored pencil, possibly a gel pencil, one that had run and become almost unreadable.

I reached to pull the envelope out of the garbage, but a sudden shiver made me pull my hand back.

Geeze, girl, that's just a soggy envelope, probably

from some school kid's idea of a joke. It's not going to bite you.

Maybe it was some kind of school kid joke—without doubt there were some pretty wild and weird kids in Jacques Station, but the envelope looked as though it had spent plenty of time under my rear window wiper, so it must have come from farther afield. Probably a plea for a cash donation, or a cheap advertising gimmick, or…

Open the damned envelope, Gracie. It's actually addressed to you. What's up with you?

Okay, I admitted to myself that this whole issue with the Wednesday group of heartbroken moms and the weird stuff going on at the halfway house group had me pretty well spooked.

So, behave like a grownup, for heaven's sake. Take a deep breath and rip the envelope open. Carefully, because it was pretty damp.

I cannot ever explain the depth of shock that washed over me at the childish writing that leapt from the page.

"Mommy, I want to come home. Why did you leave me? I'm in the woods. I'm scared. Come and find me. Becky."

I thought my heart was going to stop. *My little Becky, alone in the woods, waiting for me.*

Everything else faded. I was no longer a grown woman with a mind of her own. I was a mom with a lost and needy child. Nothing mattered now except my baby was alive and waiting for me to rescue her. I didn't stop to think, couldn't focus on anything except getting to the woods where I'd left Becky all those years ago at a birthday party.

I didn't stop to ask myself why she was there or

allow the thought that the only way she could be there was if she was buried in the woods. There was no room in my head or heart for such thoughts.

I grabbed my coat, slipped my feet into boots, and headed for my front door. I turned at the last minute and picked a soft shawl that hung in the hallway. I heard my cell phone ringing, stopping, ringing again. It didn't matter. Nothing mattered except getting to my daughter.

Becky might be cold, it's so rainy out there.

I jumped into my car, blind to everything around me except the road to the Constantine Woods and Becky. My daughter's sweet face seemed to float ahead of me, beckoning, begging…

Looking back on those moments, I know now there was a temporary madness. But my heart was longing so much to see my child that there was no rhyme or reason in my thoughts as I roared away.

****

As Fate would have it, Ben returned to my house to pick up a scarf he was sure he'd left behind on the hook beside my front door. He was surprised to find the door standing open, and a shiver of alarm ran down his spine.

As he reached for the scarf, the landline started to ring, and then the cell phone shrilled. His anxiety notched up as he saw I had been in such a rush to leave that I'd left her precious cell phone, a gadget he knew I was rarely parted from. Ben said later he felt a rush of fear for me as he regarded the shrilling phone that was an uncomfortable indicator of a sudden, precipitous departure.

He wasn't going to answer the ringing phones. He'd winced at the thought of my possible reaction to his invasion of my privacy. But after all, I had left the front door open...

"To hell with it," he muttered under his breath as he reached for the shrilling landline.

"Hello?" *Gracie is going to kill me...*

"Hello? I'm trying to reach Gracie Pelham?"

A man's voice. Ben wasn't sure whether to put the phone down or what. Was this a personal call from another man?

But the man on the other end of the line started speaking in an urgent voice. "This is John Haggarty. I'm Gracie's supervisor at the halfway house. Who am I speaking to?"

Ben identified himself and the caller continued in an even more anxious tone. "You're the police? Has anything... Is Gracie...?"

"I've just arrived at Gracie's house, but she's not here."

The man on the other end of the line took a deep, agitated breath. "I'm afraid this is very important. If she's not there, could you please find her and pass a message on to her? It's imperative she stays in her home or with friends..." The halfway house supervisor sounded rattled.

Icy fingers of fear raced down Ben's spine. What the hell had Gracie got herself into now? He took in a deep breath, trying to quell the tension in his gut.

"She's gone out, I'm afraid, and I'm not sure when she'll be back... I'm Ben Pelham, her husband. Can I take a message?"

"Her husband? I thought... Oh, never mind that now." The man on the other end of the line took in a deep breath and slowly let it out. "Are you able to get a message to her? This is urgent! You must find her and warn her! Tell her Seth Marshall has somehow managed to slip out of the closed custody area, and I'm afraid he may be looking for Gracie. It's more than likely he's heading for the U.S. border. I have officers from the OPP out searching for him, but just in case, Gracie needs to be in a safe place until this is over."

Ben's heart started to pound as he took in the message. He assured the man he'd find me, and noted the cell phone number Haggarty was calling from. "I'll let you know when I find her."

"Please do—I am very worried about Seth's intentions…"

But Ben scarcely heard the other man's words. He saw the soggy letter lying on the kitchen table and immediately guessed what was happening. His almost-ex-wife had gone haring off in hopes of finding their little girl. She'd not paused to figure out where the letter came from, or why…

Moments later, Ben was in his car, peeling away from Gracie's house while barking out orders to some of his officers to search the Constantine Woods, and to act carefully because an escaped parolee might well be armed and in those same woods.

****

Looking back, I think I must have had some form of out-of-body experience. Otherwise there's not a cat-in-hell's chance I would have fallen for some grubby, badly written note.

The nerve of the sender, thinking I would actually believe this was my daughter's handwriting! Still, I just went hurtling onwards, regardless, through the wintry-looking landscape.

But Fate or some kindly angel must have had more

wisdom than I had.

In my urgency, heart pounding, I took a country lane corner too fast, hit the icy rim of the road, and lost control of the car.

My grandma always told me I had a special angel watching over me, and that angel must have been pretty busy recently. Certainly, she was probably feeling quite dismayed as my car skidded onto the soft shoulder of the country lane, bounced back onto the hard core, skidded around in a dizzying circle, and came to a stop halfway on the road and halfway in a mass of ice-coated weeds on the edge of the road.

Fortunately, I wasn't witness to much of this—the first swerve had thrown me forwards to hit my head on the windshield with a resounding *thwap* and I lost consciousness briefly.

I'm still not sure whether to be grateful for that small mercy or not.

Speaking of small mercies, as I shook myself back into the real world, the first face I saw was Ben's, peering in through the driver's side window and, my goodness, the man looked pale as the frosty rimed road around us.

He yanked open my door and pulled me into his arms, gently hugging me and checking for broken bones. By this time, I was shaking and fighting back tears that threatened to swamp me. Ben pulled me even closer and, the next thing I knew, he was kissing me with a passion that stirred up past memories of the good times we had once had together...

When he released me, I clung to him. I couldn't believe what I had done. Not the rushing out on a wild goose chase, nor kissing my ex-husband back like my life depended on it.

And neither, it seemed, could Ben, given the angry words he was throwing at me by that time. He had some very interesting phrases to describe my stupidity and why he couldn't understand why he loved me so much, since he honestly dreaded to think what I might get up to next.

"You could have got yourself killed!" He swore a few epithets under his breath to color his view of my actions. "And not just that, you could have got someone else killed. Driving like a lunatic was bad enough, but doing it on ice, well…"

Ben recovered his equilibrium and let me out of his arms as he called for a tow truck to take my poor car to a garage in town to be checked over. He loaded me— under protest, I might say—into his car like so much luggage, brooking no argument about taking me to the hospital for a checkup.

I opened my mouth to protest that I was fine, but his dark look didn't need explanation, and I decided silence was the better part of valor and shut up.

Chapter Ten

Ben insisted that I get the bump on my head checked out in the ER, and so we spent some time in the hospital waiting room talking about the note that had been left so precariously in my rear windshield wiper. Despite tossing around a whole bunch of ideas about what it meant and where it came from, I had to finally agree with Ben that there was little, indeed, no evidence that this was anything but a prank.

"So, who among the people you know would be nasty enough to play a trick like this?" Ben asked.

I reared back. "Why does it have to be someone I know? You're a cop, which makes you one of the less popular people among the locals. People like me more than they like you, and I think the note was an attempt to get at you." I sniffed to show my sense of injustice.

But there was a niggling itch in the back of my mind, one that sent shivers along my spine. Someone had wanted me to leave my home and go in a hurry to Constantine Woods, an area of thick woodlands and, at this time of the year and weather, pretty much deserted. If I had got there, what—or who—would have been waiting there?

Certainly not my daughter.

And certainly not someone with good intent.

I started to tell Ben my feelings, but then the doctor came into the room where we'd been asked to wait. He looked tired and harassed, yet still kept a businesslike attention to detail as he asked some questions, raised an eyebrow at my story of going too fast and skidding, and then told me I was lucky not to have been more seriously hurt.

I felt a little bit like a scolded schoolkid under his serious gaze, but at the same time, I trusted the man. It was a relief when he flipped over the file he carried and announced, "You're actually a lucky young woman, Dr. Pelham. The x-rays show no internal brain damage, although I imagine you've some bruising and the beginnings of a mean headache.

"Head injuries can be dangerous things, especially to the forehead. But I'm glad to say that it looks like your skull was thick enough to absorb the worst of the blow."

I ignored the "told you so" snigger from Ben.

The doctor continued, "I suggest you rest for the remainder of the day, take a couple of painkillers, and stay off driving until you feel fully recovered. And maybe slow down on ice."

Out of the corner of my eye I saw Ben still grinning since the comment about my thick skull. He'd pay for that later…

I thanked Dr. Armand, who warned me again not to do anything for the rest of the day.

I was going to call a cab, but Ben insisted on taking me home in his car. "Yours is still being checked out at the garage, but they seem to think there's not much damage, and we'll pick it up tomorrow," he told me, guiding me along the corridor and towards where his own car was parked.

Ben started the car and put on the heater, then turned to me. His expression was very serious, and I braced myself for whatever lecture he was going to give me. I had to admit my behavior probably warranted a good lecture.

"Honestly, Ben, I can't explain why I went haring off to the woods, except that some part of my mind grabbed on to the idea that this was from Becky, or someone who knew where Becky was, and the answer was in the woods. Okay, I admit it sounds really stupid, but I wasn't thinking straight."

"It's a bad habit of yours, acting before you think," Ben snapped. "Anyhow, I hope you've learned something from this."

At that moment Ben's cell beeped and he answered it. After a few brief words, he turned to me. "There was a thorough search of that area of the woods. There was no sign that anyone, not even a dog walker, let alone a convict, had been there."

We drove back to Jacques Station in silence, and Ben insisted on coming into the house with me. He checked through it everywhere and then joined me in the kitchen.

"Tell me about this Seth character. I understand he was a member of your halfway house group?"

"How do you know about Seth?" I asked.

Ben told me about returning for his scarf and answering the call from the halfway house supervisor. "It seems this Seth left the halfway house without permission."

I felt icy fingers run down my spine. Seth had escaped from the locked isolation room?

"I feel like a total idiot. I read that note left on my car—the one you found and brought in—and somehow, I lost all sense of reality. All I could think of was that

Becky was in the woods. I didn't stop to think how she could be there, except for a brief thought that she'd been murdered and buried there by the man who'd taken her—the spot is near to where the birthday party was that she disappeared from. I can't explain it, I know it sounds so very irrational, but it was as though I'd lost my senses…"

"Why was this Seth there, in the halfway house? Or what was he in trouble for in the first place?"

I winced. "Ben, you know I can't talk about the clients…"

Ben huffed in disgust at my use of the word "client." He admonished me, "These guys aren't buying a suit or a bunch of flowers. They're jailbirds, and in the case of the ones you're working with, they're mostly men who prey on children. The worst of the worst."

I can't argue with Ben, except that I think there's a chance to save these men, teach them to handle their impulses, and so protect children, but Ben's a cop and his opinion is that anyone hurting a child should be locked up and the key thrown away.

Of course, I've always suspected that his view is colored by the disappearance of our beautiful Becky. Ben doted on our daughter, and I don't think he's ever fully gotten over her disappearance.

And neither have I. But we need to deal with the events of the present. The idea of Seth being free and able to find another victim makes my blood run cold. I explained the position to Ben.

"If he's left the halfway house, then he may be the one who put that note on my rear windshield, out of sheer mischief. He sounds like a possible candidate."

Ben was silent for a few moments, but he never took his eyes off my face. One thing about my almost-ex, Ben could read me like a book.

My home seemed peculiarly quiet and, well, not exactly empty, but quiet and cold and strange. Then I realized the McDonaghs had moved into their new digs a couple of streets away. Their chattering and clattering had become part of the background noise in my home, and I was surprised to realize that I actually missed them.

Tears sprang to my eyes. I'd gotten used to the rough and tumble of the two teenaged boys, their midnight refrigerator raids, their endless joshing and teasing. And I would miss the parents, too, especially Sandy, whose quiet chats and sensible attitude I'd grown fond of.

A sharp rat-a-tat at my front door startled me and I spilled my cup of nerve-calming herbal tea down the front of my favorite sweater when the sharp, demanding knock sounded again.

Nervous as a long-tailed cat on a porch filled with rocking chairs—a saying of my grandmother's—I peered out from behind the living room curtains before opening the door to find the owner of our local garden store, Sue Williams, standing on the step with a big smile and a beautiful floral bouquet in her arms.

"Hello, Gracie! I wanted to deliver this myself. It's a thank-you from the McDonagh family for letting them stay with you until they found a local place. I guess they were really worried about having to move away to Kingston, and it made the world of difference to them to have some extra time to find a place right here in Jacques Station."

I was momentarily overwhelmed with the spate of information. But what could I say? My heart sped up with pleasure at the gift, and tears sprang to my eyes.

"Hey, girl, don't go crying over these beautiful

flowers!"

"Wow, this is a surprise! Why, I haven't had flowers sent to me for ages…" I smiled and thanked her.

Sue gave me the bouquet, patted my hands, and wished me well as she headed back to her van.

But Ben hadn't finished with me yet. "Gracie, could you not, just for once, think before you act? I will never understand you, Gracie." He finished a third cup of coffee and stood. "I want a promise from you that you'll stay right here in the house, keep the doors and windows locked, and not go wandering off. An officer is going to check up on you as often as possible. I'm leaving you with an alarm gadget—push this button if there's any sign of a problem and fifty officers will be here in minutes."

I could feel my face burning with shame. Ben was right, I did act like an idiot sometimes, without thinking. "I didn't know Seth had got away from the halfway house."

Ben expressed his view of my common sense with a string of expletives that made my face burn even more. But I didn't have any answer. Ben was right. I'd been a fool.

"How would this bastard know where to find you, or that you had a child named Becky? I doubt that's information just left lying around for anyone to read."

I chewed my bottom lip, a habit I have when stressed.

"I noticed Seth seemed to have information about me that he shouldn't have, so I checked and found out he had done some work in the office where the files are kept. He may have found some time to sneak a peek into the staff files."

"And be willing to use it against you. He was taking a chance, though, thinking you would hightail it to a remote woodland just on the off chance your child was there." Ben spoke softly, his expression gentle.

"I don't know, Ben. He must have found some way to research where I lived and what the surroundings were like. And he would have seen from the file that Becky disappeared from a party on a playground near the woods..." Hot tears stung my cheeks, but inside I was filled with rage.

Ben was pacing up and down by my kitchen table, deep in thought. I expected anger from him, but he was calm and reasonable.

"Are you sure John Haggarty said Seth had found a way to leave the locked area of the halfway house? I mean, he was supposed to be in solitary lockup," I couldn't imagine how the paroled inmate could have got away from the halfway house.

Ben surprised me by moving over and putting his arms around me. "Gracie. I know you believe you can somehow save these people from themselves, and I think you believe that one day one of your 'clients' will tell you where Becky is, safe and sound.

"But we have to deal with reality, and right now, our reality is that a bad actor like Seth Marshall would rather die than give up his freedom now he's out."

I knew he was right. In fact, I felt a bit foolish, because of all the years I'd spent working with pedophiles, always hoping that one day, someone would have information that would lead to my daughter. Dead or alive...

I shook myself. Time to stop daydreaming. I swallowed hard against my tears, moved out of the warm shelter of Ben's arms, and looked him straight in the eyes. "The note, if it came from Seth, was obviously not written by a young child. I can't imagine how Seth could have made it here from Kingston—maybe he hitched a lift, but the weather is horrible. The writer claims Becky is in Constantine Woods. I don't see Seth getting all the way here or having the skills to plot something like this."

I said as much, but Ben's second in command contacted him before this turned into a full-scale war. "It seems the officers have searched the entire area of the woods and there's no evidence anyone has been there in the last couple of days. They fanned out through the woods and, as you could expect in this freezing cold weather, it's pretty well deserted."

I struggled to swallow my disappointment. "So this was probably a wild goose chase? An attempt to divert attention?"

Ben shrugged. "The likeliest answer is exactly that—this Seth character wants time to get as far away as possible from Kingston and the halfway house, and he's pointing everyone's search to the woods here. In the meantime, he's probably hopping across the border into the U.S."

I chewed on that idea. "But without a passport?"

"We're checking to see if he has a passport, in his name or a fake one. But the fact is that there are ways to get across the border without involving officialdom." Ben shrugged, not willing to commit himself without further facts. Once a cop, always a cop.

I was so tired, but a sense of relaxation settled in on my mind, with Ben hovering around me like I was fragile. I appreciated his concern, but right now, I really needed alone time.

I was suddenly swamped with exhaustion, which I inadvertently transmitted to Ben with a huge, jaw-cracking yawn.

He smiled. "I think I should take you up to bed," he said, then I swear the man blushed as he realized what he'd said.

"I mean, I don't want you to get a dizzy spell going up those stairs, so I will walk you up. Nothing more than that," he added, making his meaning clear.

I wasn't sure whether I was disappointed or not. But one thing was sure, and that was that this counselor wasn't ready to deal with the feelings, the suggestible feelings, flowing between her and her ex.

"I have a new client coming in early tomorrow morning, and just a word of warning—your favorite old lady, the one who surprised you when you were here a few days ago with an offer you almost couldn't refuse, will also be coming in later in the morning."

My big, strong almost-ex-husband actually blushed at the memory of Mrs. LeBlanc's naughty comments to him. I know the older lady just enjoyed making him blush, and I couldn't hold back a smile.

Anyhow, whatever his feelings were, he hightailed it out to his car with a final warning to keep my doors locked, not to answer to strangers, and call him or Allie if I felt ill or dizzy.

Chapter Eleven

"Hey, girlfriend—I saw the police cars over at the woods, and then again at your place—what gives? Is everything all right with you?" Allie sounded really worried on the phone.

I could barely keep my eyes open, but I knew a long girl talk with my best friend would be the best medicine.

"Thanks for calling, Allie. Listen, things have been a bit crazy over here. I'd love to have a nice chat with you, but first I really need a hot shower to wake me up. I'll leave the front door on the latch, and maybe you'd pop over in half an hour or so?"

Allie assured me she'd "be there with bells on" and bring some chocolate chip cookies, just for comfort. Allie baked like an angel, and my mouth watered at the very mention of her cookies, so I was smiling as I stepped into the hot shower.

There's nothing quite like lathering up your body and doctoring your hair with sweet lavender-smelling shampoo and conditioner to aid relaxation.

I lingered a little longer than I intended, and once out of the shower quickly pulled on underwear and a fluffy sweater. My slacks were still in the bedroom. The hair dryer took a few minutes, and as I turned it off I heard the big front door open downstairs.

I opened the bathroom door and called down to my friend that I'd need a minute, and would she please put the kettle on for tea?

I went through the connecting door into my bedroom and didn't hear her answer, but suddenly the door was flung open with a crash as it hit the inside wall. I swiveled around in surprise—Allie generally kept to proper privacy manners.

But my stomach lurched as I took in the face of the intruder.

Not Allie. Nothing like my well-meaning, good-hearted friend.

Instead, a monster stood there, grinning from ear to ear as he surveyed my partially undressed state.

"Well, well, well," Seth said, "Don't you make a pretty picture!"

My heart was pounding. I knew I didn't have a chance to fight this man, twice my weight and a good ten inches taller than me. And muscular...

I think I'm going to vomit.

I bit my terror back and went on the offensive. "Seth, what the hell do you think you're doing? Do you want to go back to jail? Because I'll see you there, or in hell..." Brave words, but the squeaky tremble in my voice gave me away.

"I thought you only liked little kids," I squawked as he lumbered towards me, forcing me to scramble backwards until my knees were against the bed. All that time he never lost that hideous grin.

I suddenly understood what the meaning of "blood running cold" really felt like.

"I think I can make an exception for you, little lady. I think you'll be squealing just like a little girl when I'm inside you..."

I seemed to lose the ability to move, to run, to save

myself, as the bastard pushed me backwards onto my bed, his hands grabbing at the towel around my waist, then slipping brutally between my legs, his grin growing wider as he realized I was still mostly undressed…

His touch brought me back to reality and I scratched at his face with my fingernails, but he just grabbed my arms and pushed them above my head.

And all the time he never lost that grin.

Suddenly, his expression turned from wicked lust to shock, his eyes rolled back in his head, and he collapsed on me. That's when I saw my friend, Allie, all five feet two of her, looking flushed as she raised the metal nightstand lamp over her head and whacked Seth again.

"Just making sure he's not going to wake up any time soon," she muttered, her eyes glittering with anger and triumph.

Yep, that's my friend. The warrior vicar…

I didn't realize I'd said the words aloud as I pushed Seth's unconscious body off me and pulled myself off the bed. It was probably the result of shock, but when Ben rushed into the room…well, his face was a picture.

"What the hell…?" he muttered.

"Ben, darling, I'd like to introduce you to Seth. Seth is a pedophile, only he seems to like women, too," I said, moving to put my arms around Allie. "Allie saved me from…a fate worse than death."

And we both giggled wildly as I slipped my favorite jogging pants on. Shock.

Then I began to cry.

It didn't take Ben long to realize what had happened. I don't think I have ever seen the man so angry. I think if he'd not been a cop, he might well have murdered Seth on the spot.

Instead, he pulled out his radio and called in two of his officers. Then he handcuffed Seth's hands behind his back, very tightly. The man was moaning and just starting to realize what had happened…what he'd done…

Allie put her arms around me, and we managed to get down the stairs. I wasn't crying any more, but I was mad and wanted to go back upstairs to kick the living daylights out of my attacker. Allie and Ben held me back.

"If you beat him up, he might just seek a lawyer who will send a warrant for you, alleging that you attacked him."

A short time later, Ben's officers arrived and soon escorted Seth, who was looking pretty dazed, down the stairs and out of my house.

"We're going to have to smudge the house, you know," insisted Allie, whose grandparents on her mother's side were First Nations people.

I agreed. I'd have agreed to anything if it might take away the memory of Seth's groping hands, and my own feelings of absolute helplessness. I could not remember ever feeling like that before, and it might take me a while to regain my feelings of safety.

Ben came back into the room and put his arms around me. I was waiting for one of his lectures about the kind of men I was working with, but instead he squeezed me tightly against him, then let me go.

"Allie, will you be able to stay with Gracie? I have to go to the station and see this bastard safely put in the cells and all the correct paperwork done."

"Of course. In fact, we're going to have a little drink of wine, then go upstairs and clear up the bedroom and any traces that monster may have left behind of his evil."

Allie's voice reflected the anger she was feeling.

Well, well! I was seeing a whole new side of my religious friend. Allie has been a church minister most of her adult life, following in the footsteps of her father, who had been minister at the local church for years before his retirement.

I didn't know how I would ever thank my friend for her brave attack on that monster, for saving me from, well, a fate worse than death, and for acting so swiftly to save me. She didn't pause to think of the religious belief of turning the other cheek, and I would always admire her ability to see when violence in the name of saving another person might be justified.

****

Not surprisingly, I didn't slept well that night. Even though Allie stayed late to see me settled, and, to my surprise, Ben stayed the night. Seems he had arrived in the wee small hours, driven Allie back to the manse, and then returned to check on me.

I must have fallen asleep after the wine Allie had fed me—for purely medicinal reasons, she insisted—but I had no idea of any of these things.

When morning came, I was awakened by Ben with a cup of coffee. He told me he'd slept in the big old armchair, downstairs in the living room—the chair that had once belonged to my grandmother—and according to him, it had been pretty comfortable.

But he'd probably slept lightly, too, with the door open, one ear always listening in case I made any sounds of distress.

"Sorry to wake you up so soon, Gracie, but I'll have to go the station. There's a ton of paperwork to be done there, as well as more time interviewing some people.

How are you feeling? Do you think you'll be okay if I leave to get some paperwork done at the station?"

I rubbed the last remnants of sleep out of my eyes. "Did you talk to John Haggarty about…about what… happened with Seth?" I had to ask. I had to know where that monster was currently lurking, if he was still around, polluting the pleasant village atmosphere…

Ben sat on the edge of my bed, his fingers gently pushing the hair off my flushed cheeks. "I am so sorry this happened to you, Gracie," he said. "An attack like that is one of the most frightening things that can happen to a woman."

I remembered the shocked look on Seth's face as he was marched away. "I think maybe it was a pretty shocking experience for Seth, too, especially after my tiny friend Allie hit him with the lamp!"

I couldn't help the thin smile that hovered on my lips.

Ben leaned forward and planted a kiss on my forehead, taking me by surprise. "Don't worry about Seth, Gracie. He's safely in the local police jail and about to be driven down to Kingston. He'll be brought before the courts, and it's unlikely he'll be a free man for a long time to come."

"Will I need to give evidence?" I hated the idea of standing up in court, answering questions that could only highlight my own weakness in not being able to prevent what happened. But I didn't reveal those thoughts to Ben.

"Well, first off, he's going to be remanded back to jail to finish out his original sentence. His days of having the relative freedom of being in the halfway house are over.

"There will be a trial, and you will be probably called to testify—along with your friend, Allie, I imagine. But that's all up to the lawyers. And the courts take a very dim view of what happened here." He leaned over me and brushed a quick kiss onto my forehead. He still wore the same aftershave as he'd had when we were married, and the scent brought back so many memories. And feelings.

Get over it, Gracie girl. He's just feeling sorry for you, and remember—he's the one who asked for the divorce.

Then he was gone, and I was left wondering just what that was all about. Was there a reason he hadn't yet signed the final divorce papers, other than being too busy?

I took a deep breath, then lay back against my pillows with the coffee he had brought. It was pointless to try and second-guess a man, especially one as complicated as he was.

Chapter Twelve

I couldn't hang around in bed all morning, even though I felt like hibernating away from everyone and everything to recover from the previous day.

But I was committed to running the bereavement class, and I knew from experience that it acts as a lifeline for some of the mothers struggling to come to terms with the loss of their children—particularly, the ones whose deaths were due to drug overdoses or violence, the sort of deaths often thought of as pointless, unnecessary, and totally heartbreaking.

So, I pulled myself out from under the lovely warm, quilted bedspread and took a quick shower. Drying my hair and choosing some clothes actually seemed to calm me down. *Everyday normalcy, I guess.*

I arrived at the church basement, where we held the meetings, just as several of the participants were coming in.

To my surprise, Sophia Scott was there already. I had not expected to see her again, especially as I told her she would not gain anything from the group and needed some private counselling to sort out her attitude.

She flashed me a brief smile, but I couldn't help feeling suspicious of her intent, and I was pretty uncomfortable as we set up the chairs in the drab old basement room we used.

Sophia's claim of "I get mad, and I get even" was

still caught in my thoughts, and I felt a real need to keep this woman at arm's length.

As group leader, I moderate, coax, question, and reflect their words back to those who spoke them, in hopes they'll find their way through the dark maze and into the light. Looking around the now diminished group, I realized several of the participants had cried off. I had an idea they could not deal with the anger and sheer meanness demonstrated by Sophia Scott and the two women who appeared to be actively supporting her.

"Sophia, I believe I asked you not to come to group until you were ready to participate in a way that didn't upset everyone here," I said, keeping my voice nicely moderated so as not to give away the fact I wanted to slap the smug grin off the woman's face.

I looked to the other two, Vera and Elsie, hoping for support. Or at least some sign that they did not harbor the kind of bitter, violent anger that poured from Sophia.

They looked back at me with a dark, hard look that made my shiver. Then Vera started to cry.

"Gracie, I'm sorry—I don't know what to do now…"

Sophia stood up and pushed a hand against Vera's chest. "Shut up, you whiney bitch. Either grow a spine or get away from me." The harsh words just brought on a greater flood of tears.

"Sophia, that's enough!" I was afraid the shoving would erupt into a full-blown fight.

"Quit wailing—you were all full of doing this, of cleaning up the drug dealers who killed our kids. Now you're just a whiney baby who won't stand up for your own son."

I gasped at the harsh, spiteful words. I was about to

order Sophia to leave immediately, including Elsie in my glare. "You should leave, too, Elsie, if you feel this group isn't enough for you."

Sophia stormed out, with Elsie following. She stopped at the door and gave me a look I couldn't fathom, almost as if she was going to cry, too, and then she was gone. The door slammed so hard behind her the glass in the windows rattled.

The only three other women still here, besides a weeping Vera, were Janey Barnes, Rainey Briggs, Julia Scammell, and they all exchanged looks.

Then, in one accord, they all three stood up and went and put their arms around Vera, effectively bringing her back into the group.

The action brought tears to my eyes.

In fact, I thought about this lovely act of kindness and acceptance. I would have to describe the moment to Allie—such an act of kindness and forgiveness would warm her heart, too.

But I was still troubled about the behavior of Sophia and Elsie. There was something—as I drove home, I struggled to put my finger on just what it was I was trying to understand. It seemed that I had murder on my mind, because it was the recent deaths of the three young men that dominated my thoughts.

Could it be that Sophia was involved in the violence against the young drug dealers?

But something wasn't right, and I couldn't quite put my finger on it.

Or maybe I simply didn't want to bring my idea out into the light for inspection.

****

Surprise!

I arrived home to find Ben yet again sitting outside my door in his car. As I parked and got a clear look at the man, I could see he was pale with exhaustion. He looked like he hadn't slept in a week. That's my Ben—he won't stop until he gets the job done.

But in this case, it was pretty obvious that getting the job done wasn't going to be easy. And the very idea that someone would get away with murdering three young men just sent shivers down my spine.

I got out of my car and went and tapped on the window of Ben's. He jerked and I suddenly realized he'd been dozing.

"Come on, sleepyhead—you're not going to catch the bad guys while you're asleep in your police car," I teased.

Then I unlocked my house door and sauntered inside, sure that my soon-to-be-ex would follow me—or the scent of good coffee—inside.

I'd got the coffeemaker buzzing and gurgling by the time Ben walked in, sloughed off his heavy jacket, and flopped down onto one of my antique kitchen chairs.

"Take it easy on that chair, Ben! It took me a long time to find all six that matched."

Ben shrugged apologetically and sat up straighter. I was shocked to see just how tired he looked, under the bright central ceiling light.

"Have you eaten anything today?"

Ben bit his lip. "I can't remember—I think I ate a couple of Tim Horton donuts sometime around six this morning…"

I sighed loudly. "Look, maybe you need a babysitter! You're old enough to know when you're hungry and to get some food."

But he looked so pathetic that I gave in and placed a dish of bran flakes with some fresh blueberries, the milk jug, and a spoon in front of him, along with a large-sized mug of coffee.

He muttered his thanks, and I swear the man inhaled the food and coffee right before my eyes. I offered him a refill and he nodded.

"I didn't get much sleep last night, and I left your house very early to join in the patrols with my fellow officers, just driving around, keeping an eye on things," he said through a mouthful of cereal.

"Did anything happen?" I couldn't resist asking.

Ben shook his head. "No, it was all quiet. Well, aside from a bunch of kids smoking behind the school, and an elderly woman out calling for her cat…"

I sat up with a gasp. "Was she very elderly?"

"Yes. and the cat was positively ancient."

"That must have been Millie, my neighbor from across the road. Was she okay?"

"WPC Robbins was very good with her, helped her catch that mangy cat and took them both safely home. That was about four a.m. and the most exciting thing that happened all night."

We sat in silence for a few minutes, basking in the heat from the small kitchen woodstove.

"I think we're going to get snow soon," I commented, just to make conversation before Ben actually nodded off. I had never seen the man so tired, ever.

"I thought snow would deter these young guys from being out all night, selling whatever drugs they can get their hands onto. Anyhow, it was all quiet last night. Word must have got out about the police being around. I don't know their sources for the drugs, but I will find out. I will track them down…"

"So were you here for a reason, besides the free food and coffee?"

Ben sat up in his seat, suddenly looking wide awake. "I came here to tell you, to warn you, about what we've learned about the autopsies of the three dead drug-dealing youths."

My stomach roiled. I wasn't at all sure I wanted to hear what he was going to tell me.

"According to the postmortems, all three had experienced multiple stab wounds. It's almost like a ritual slaughter."

I was stunned into silence. What type of maniac stabs someone multiple times? "The attacker must have been wildly angry to stab so many times. Either that, or he was so crazy—or even scared—that he didn't know what he was doing." I was basically thinking out loud as my mind tried to come to terms with such an attack. "Or—and I hope to God not—it could have been a ritual, if all three were killed in the same way."

Ben was silent for several minutes.

When he spoke, I found it hard to believe what I was hearing.

"Gracie, we've thought of that, and that number of stabbings is an attacker out of control. The thing is, Gracie, there were three stab wounds…and three different weapons were used. Almost as if it was…like I said, a ritual."

"The killer must have been very angry…"

"The wounds were made with three different blades…so it could have been three different killers. Or one very angry one."

My blood ran cold. Who, in our little community or the small surrounding villages could be so…so crazily insane as to carry out a ritual murder? Three ritual murders of young men? My mind reeled back to the previous thoughts that had haunted me. No, it couldn't be…

We were silent for some minutes before I tentatively said: "Ben, could there have been more than one attacker?"

"Three attackers? Yes, that's possible. We're looking at every possibility. But that would be pretty unusual. Honestly, Gracie, I'm not sure where this is going. What worries me is that if someone—or several someones—carried out attacks like this, then where will they stop? If it's revenge, they might feel they've had their dues, and it will be over. But if it's a ritual—well, I have no idea where that takes us."

"You mean, there could be other similar killings? Like when there's a full moon or some other crazy stuff? Surely not, not here in Jacques Station—because if someone that crazy lives amongst us, I am sure we'd have noticed that craziness."

"I know that's something you'd like to believe, Gracie. But three young men have been stabbed to death, and no one knows anything. No one has seen or heard anything."

As Ben got up to leave, I hugged him tightly. "Take care out there, Ben," I whispered as he slipped on his coat and left my house.

Chapter Thirteen

I had only one client booked for that afternoon, an older man who was having difficulty coping with his wife's cancer diagnosis.

"I try. Every day I try to keep a smile on my face and keep her spirits up. Chemo is hell. She feels absolutely awful, and there's still a series of radiation treatments to come. That's if she's strong enough to take it.

"Gracie, I'm not sure how we'll cope. I can't lose her. I hate to see her suffering through the treatment, and I know that if she stops the treatment, she'll die for sure. The cancer will kill her. And how could I go on, without my Betsy?"

We had the same conversation every time Bill Saunders came for an appointment. I knew he wasn't expecting any answers from me, indeed, all he really wanted was someone to tell his fears and feelings too. The couple had been married for sixty years, had suffered the death of their eldest daughter in a car accident, and their youngest child, a son, had killed himself while hooked on drugs. Bill and Betty were alone in the world to cope with their fears of pain and loss.

We sat for fifty minutes while Bill talked, and I listened, or we both sat silently as the poor man tried to work up the strength to return home to the woman he loved and sit with her while the cancer continued to ravage her body and the treatments drained her strength.

And when the time was over, I always hugged Bill. Maybe it's not considered professional, but those few moments of contact were all Bill had now and seemed to bolster his resolve to go home and sit with his wife.

When Bill was gone and I was at last alone in my home, I brewed a cup of herbal tea and went into the small room off the kitchen. This room was more like a conservatory, filled with thriving plants and sunshine and peace.

I must have been sitting there on the white wicker settee, staring out onto the garden that embraced the house at the back and sides, for more than an hour while I considered the horrors I had learned from Ben.

Finally, I allowed myself to think of the one possibility I found more horrific than any I'd discussed with Ben. For in the back of my mind, I thought I knew who the killer was. Or killers. But my heart was having problems believing what my mind kept telling me. But the murders were definitely on my mind, and I couldn't shake the feeling that their shadow was much too close to home.

Finally, when I couldn't ruminate any longer about the possibility of an issue that I had no factual reasons to believe, I decided to go across the road and visit Millie and her cat.

I took a casserole out of my freezer. I like to keep a few cooked meals available for the many, many times I don't feel like cooking when I get home. I wrapped it in a padded cotton carrier that I bought at one of the church craft sales. The carrier was perfect for the job I needed it to do.

By now it was almost dusk, and I briefly considered it probably wasn't a good idea to be wandering the streets with only a casserole dish for a weapon if crazed killers were lurking in our little village. The fact that I had a thought like that made me smile.

Millie opened her door cautiously, keeping the weathered screen door closed until she recognized who was at her door.

"Gracie! What a lovely surprise! I am sure Maxie will be pleased to see you, too! Just let me grab him. You know how naughty he can be, wanting to be outside and hunting mice and rats all the time."

I hadn't intended to stay, just to drop off the meal for the old lady I knew didn't bother to do much cooking.

Unless it was a meal for that mangy old cat. I do believe that old cat actually kept Millie alive, a companion to love and live for and take care of.

She invited me in for a cup of tea, and we sat and chatted a little while about ordinary, everyday goings on. After all, when a good chunk of the village you live in has been burned to the ground, there's generally a lot to talk about and a lot to compare notes about.

I didn't mention the murders. The old lady had enough to be anxious about without adding to the list.

At last, I could see that Millie was close to nodding off. I also noticed that her cat was sitting on the kitchen counter, apparently guarding the casserole dish. Cats have a great sense of smell, and that mangy, much-loved old thing knew what the dish held before his owner could possibly guess. His look said it all—this is meat stew…this is mine.

We said our goodbyes, and without wanting to alarm Millie, I felt I should mention casually that there had been some rough stuff in the neighborhood, and she should be watchful about opening her door to strangers or going out at night.

"Give me a call if anything worries you, or if you need anything," I told her and left for the quiet of my own home.

It was getting late, and I was tired after the events of the day, so I decided on an early night with my library book and a glass of wine to help me sleep.

But when I finally finished my drink and put the lights out—after a quick trip downstairs to check for the third time that all my doors and windows were locked—sleep was reluctant to claim me.

I tossed and turned, going over and over again all the little things I'd noticed, things that were disturbing but couldn't possibly point to someone I knew being a murderer.

And certainly not a multiple killer committing multiple murders.

Sleep was slow in coming.

Chapter Fourteen

I woke up with the morning sun blazing into my eyes as if giving me an up-and-at-'em call to action. My first thought was, *How come this wintry sun is so bright?* And my second thought was, *Gee, it's bright because it's gone ten o'clock and I've overslept.*

Fortunately, I had no client appointments today, and no need to go to either the halfway house group or the bereavement group. That thought made me feel a lot better. A whole day off!

So I took my time with a nice hot shower and got dressed in some casual jeans and a fluffy warm sweater. I hadn't anything planned for the day, but I knew in my heart I had a major problem to deal with and I seriously lacked any ideas of how to go about that dealing.

Oh, I wasn't planning to solve any crimes or anything like that, but I did have some thoughts I needed to run by someone who wasn't involved.

But first I had things to do. Mundane things, like about ten loads of laundry—I hadn't caught up with the bedding and towels used by the McDonagh family yet, as well as a pile of my own clothing. And it was time to pull out some of my bigger, warmer winter clothes and give them a run through the laundry to make sure I was prepared for the downturn in the weather.

I never purchase any clothing that needs to be dry cleaned or even babied in any other way. If it can't be thrown in the washer and transferred to the dryer without sniveling and whingeing, well, it's not for me.

Except for a couple of much loved, very expensive sweaters that I guard with my life, and I pet and baby those and avoid wearing them to any event where I might accidently spill food or drink on them. In the case of an accident like that, well, it would be a dry-cleaning issue, and I try to avoid that. The nearest dry-cleaning service is in Kingston, and that's quite a drive.

So, I anticipated several hours running down and up the stairs to the basement, where the elderly washing machine and the spanking new dryer ruled the roost.

It took me until midafternoon to have everything washed, aside from a final run of sheets which I figured could wait a little until the next day. In my experience, bedsheets are not generally given to hysterics if they're not first in the wash.

Then I spent some time chasing the dust bunnies and hunting out abandoned dishes and cups and glasses. My excuse is that sometimes I have guests and they're not always too fussy about where they pop their crockery and cutlery down.

That's my excuse and I'm sticking to it.

Anyway, by this time it was three o'clock and I was famished. Lunch had fallen by the wayside while I played the good housewife. Ha! Like I'd ever been like that. Don't ever ask Ben how good a housekeeper I'd been—the man has a terrible tendency to tell the truth.

All that exercise later and I was starving, so I made a couple of pieces of toast with honey and a large cup of tea. I fired up my computer to see what was going on in the world—none of it good, most of it depressing, except for a cute story about a guy who rescued a moose that had fallen into a lake. I thought moose liked to wallow in water, but it appears this one was either a bit stupid or had ventured too far out into deeper water.

Ah, well, at least the moose survived, and the rescuer was pretty good-looking, too.

I knew I needed to talk to someone with a sane view of the world, and my first thought was my counselling supervisor. I was still crunching on toast and speculating on the idiocy of the world when Jack answered his telephone. Or his answering machine answered, and for a moment I was relieved not to have to try explaining my thoughts to him.

Because I had a better person in mind—my friend Allie was the most sensible person I knew, and she was probably the very best person to relieve me of the suspicions burdening me.

I called her to make sure she didn't have any work-related issues to deal with this late afternoon.

"You're in luck, kiddo! Today is a quiet day, all day—fingers crossed. Come on over, I would love to see you. And by the way, you'll be happy to hear that Tina got that job in Peterborough. She's away from home from Wednesday to Saturday, so it's safe for you to come around."

"Do I come across as that much of a coward?" I asked. "I'm not afraid of Tina! At least not when I know she's not there."

Allie's laugh sounded all the way through the Bell Canada satellite and into my cell phone.

Allie had set up the seats on the manse rear sunporch, where we could sit in reasonable warmth and enjoy the wintry sunlight, provided we kept our jackets on. It was late October, after all.

We sipped orange juice, and I told her about the events I'd been involved in over the past few days, and my worries about the murders of the three young men.

"I know they were dealing drugs, and never in my life would I exonerate them for that. But at the same time, drug dealing isn't a capital crime, but someone seems to think they deserved to be executed."

I saw the color drain from my friend's face as she took in what I was saying.

"That can't be so, Gracie! Not…not executions? Really, this is Jacques Station, not Toronto or New York City or…well, it just isn't."

I didn't tell her I had thought exactly the same thing, until I had talked to Ben and heard the facts from him. We sat in silence for a while, just relaxing and enjoying the peace of the day, watching the red and gold leaves fluttering to the ground from the trees that surrounded the manse.

After a time, I blurted out the idea that had been bothering me since yesterday's talk with Ben.

"Allie—do you think it's possible that a woman could be a killer? Like maybe killing these young guys? The drug dealers?"

Allie raised her eyebrows. "Come on, Gracie, why would you think that? No! Hold that thought. It's almost teatime. Would you like some macaroni and cheese? I can reheat it in the microwave."

"Sure, if that comes with a glass of wine." I really wasn't sure my stomach could deal with food right now, but I was willing to try. Anything I didn't have to cook myself always sounded good to me.

Allie turned to take a close look at me. "Were you drinking before you got here, Gracie? I mean, whatever would put the idea in your mind that women were killing people?"

"It's just that, well…oh, never mind."

"Is it because Tina is away, and the peace and freedom is going to your head? Or maybe the peace and the wine are going to your head." Allie was grinning at me. She knew how much I detested her lover. I could never get used to the idea that my kind and generous best friend would have someone like Tina in her life.

She told me to sit quietly and think about things while she went into the manse kitchen and warmed up some mac and cheese in the microwave.

She brought the food out on two plates, nicely decorated with tomato quarters and a few leaves of some herb I didn't recognize but it was very tasty.

Then we sat in silence, eating, sipping wine, and watching as darkening clouds scuttled across the sky.

As the afternoon progressed, the clouds were tinged with glorious pink, and then the sky segued into an incredible scarlet and gold as the sun slunk down towards the horizon. Sunset would arrive soon as a reminder that winter wasn't far away.

Eventually, I interrupted our pleasant silence. I turned to Allie with the question I'd been worrying around in my head since Ben's visit yesterday.

"I know it sounds crazy and farfetched, but I've worked with women whose children have been hurt or worse. Some react like lionesses, filled with anger and a desire to…well, I don't know…" I couldn't bring myself to say the word "murder."

Allie sat quietly for a few minutes, and I knew my friend was deep in thought. As a church minister she had seen both the good and the bad in people, and she knew the damage that could be done.

Finally, she bit her lip and turned to me. "I think you are very stressed out with everything that's been happening. We're not used to such violence in our little village, and I think we're all a bit loopy trying to come to terms with the aftermath of the fire and now the shocking murders that have impinged on our little village and the general area. To say nothing of the attack on yourself by that horrible escaped convict.

"And for what it's worth, I can see some mothers going crazy with grief and shock and punching or otherwise trying to harm anyone who might have hurt their child. But it would be a spur-of-the-moment thing. It's just not something I have a lot of knowledge of. Thank goodness."

We sat quietly again until the sky darkened, enjoying the calm, the country quiet, and the fading colors cast in the sky by the setting sun and rising moon.

"You know, I feel terrible about this, but I'm glad Tina is going to work in Peterborough and will only be back a few days a week. I've missed seeing you, my friend, and missed our Friday night talks and movies and…well, everything."

Allie put her glass down and turned to me with a hug.

"I've missed you, I've missed our weekly get-togethers and our talks," she said with a smile. "Overcooked pizza and cheap wine, I do miss—and most of all, I miss your company."

It was so good to catch up with my best buddy, and a relief to know our friendship had survived the impact of Tina's jealousy.

There was a smile on my face as I walked home

through the gathering dark.

Back in my own quiet home, I still felt troubled. Despite the wine and the macaroni cheese—or maybe because of the wine and the macaroni cheese—I tossed and turned as sleep eluded me.

In my mind I was going over and over the little things, again. I noticed the things that were disturbing but couldn't possibly point to someone I worked with, or a client, or a neighbor, or a friend in Jacques Station.

Nothing I knew for certain pointed to someone I knew being a murderer—or murderess. Or did it?

Daylight comes late to Ontario mornings as winter closes in, but the dark was fading into morning before I fell asleep with troubled thoughts still running in my mind.

But I did come to one conclusion—I must take some time to reexamine my thoughts and then, perhaps, to talk to Ben about what seemed to be an idea too awful even to bring out into the light.

Chapter Fifteen

I had a new client coming early this afternoon, a woman whose name was unfamiliar. Unlike most of my clients, Anita Furlong had made an appointment by email through my service, so I had an idea of what kind of difficulty she wanted to discuss with me.

It's unusual, as I generally liked a few words with a prospective client before agreeing to see her or him.

Sometimes, although rarely, it was better to have a chat with a person to be sure we were a good fit for counselling, or if I should send that person to another therapist who might specialize in a specific issue and be more helpful to the client.

As it turned out, if I had known what this woman was about, I would have refused to see her. In fact, I would have refused to let her cross the threshold of my home, and I definitely wouldn't have sicced her onto any other counsellor I know.

I had a couple of hours to spare before she was due to arrive, so I spent some time doing the everyday things that had to be done—more laundry, for one thing, and cleaning the kitchen, chasing the dust bunnies under my bed, and spraying some nice, scented polish on the furniture to give it a shine.

And vacuuming—don't forget the vacuuming. I have mostly hardwood floors—one of the joys of having an older home—but there are several scatter rugs in the living room and dining room, and oriental weave rugs in the kitchen and bedrooms.

As my housekeeping had always been a bit haphazard, I had to do some catching up, and I didn't really have a routine. I'll be honest—I was pretty well bushed by the time my house had the kind of sparkly-clean look that was always there when grandmother was in charge.

I'd just enough time for a quick shower to clean and relax me, after all the hard work, before my new client was due to arrive. I have to say I was curious about her, because the operator who called from my service with the appointment said the client lived some distance away and was travelling to see me because she had heard of my work and had decided I was the person she wanted to see.

I admit I felt a bit flattered and was looking forward to meeting Ms. Furlong in person. Oh, how foolish an unsuspecting counsellor can be!

And it looked on the surface as though we could have a good relationship and do some useful work on whatever Ms. Furlong's counselling problem was.

When she arrived, driving an expensive car and dressed in a matching coat and dress with tall boots that would have cost a mortgage payment on a family home, she was obviously a woman of means.

"I have looked forward to meeting you for some time, Gracie—I can call you Gracie, can't I?" she said as she slipped out of her very expensive label coat and proceeded to walk down my hallway, snow dropping from her boots onto my lovely oak floors.

I was about to ask her to remove them, but she was already in full chatter mode.

"What a lovely place you have here, for a village home! I do love these older homes, especially if one is of limited means."

Ouch! What's with the "limited means"? I was just about to pull her up on her rudeness when she turned to me with a tight smile on her face.

"I understand you still try to see Ben, your ex-husband, at every opportunity you get? Well, dear, don't get your hopes up. Ben and I have been seeing each other for some time. Now, I'm sure you would like to have him sniffing around at your heels like a pet puppy dog, but you're making a big mistake."

I must have been standing there with my mouth open, trying to take in what this woman was telling me. Ben was seeing her? Ben was in a serious relationship with this unpleasant woman?

I felt a sudden shot of something like pain in my heart.

"You should know that Ben has been with me for months now. He's told me how you cling to him, and how he's been seeing you only because he's trying to solve a crime, a crime in which he thinks you may have some guilty part. So, in order not to break your heart further, I thought I should tell you what is really going on. Ben has popped the question and is shopping for a ring at this very moment. I'm warning you to keep away from him. He's much too soft-hearted to tell you himself to get lost and keep out of our lives, so I thought I would take that task from him."

I finally found my voice and could speak without choking on my words. "How dare you come into my home and say these things? My relationship with Ben has been purely businesslike since we parted ways. As a counsellor I have been able to discuss a series of very serious crimes with him and offer the police some suggestions to solving them. I think you had better get out of my house before I call for a police officer to remove you."

The woman laughed in my face. "Good attempt at seeming nonchalant, honey, but you know in your heart that I'm telling the truth. No matter how much you want him, Ben will never return to you. It's me he loves."

Anita Furlong slipped into her coat, picked up her designer handbag, and with a last sneering grin, walked briskly out of my house.

I stood staring after her for what felt like an hour but was probably only a few minutes. And then the tears came. I really didn't want to believe Anita Furlong. I have more faith in Ben than to think he'd string me along.

But when I thought about it, when had Ben ever behaved in a way that might suggest he wanted to return to me? And what claim did I really have on him?

Except for not finalizing the divorce, which I supposed could be put down to his being busy and also keeping a businesslike stance, I couldn't think of any time that he had maybe suggested, by word or deed, that he wished us to be a couple again.

I slammed the heavy front door shut so hard that it seemed to make the house tremble. Then I went upstairs and threw myself on the bed for a good cry.

By now it was supper time, but my stomach was still reeling from the interview with Anita Furlong, and the idea of food was, well, awful. It hit me with the sudden strength of a heavy truck that I had actually been hoping somehow Ben and I would find our way back together.

No matter how much I denied it, I now had to admit the truth to myself.

Usually, in a situation like this, a smart woman turns to her best friend so they can have a pity party. But for some reason I wasn't ready to tell even Allie, my very best friend in the world, of the awful sorrow and humiliation I was feeling.

And even when Allie called to see if I wanted to get together and watch a horror movie—the networks were putting them on early this October—I told her I was overwhelmed with work after getting a new client, and I'd meet up with her another day.

I was still struggling with my thoughts on who the murderer or murderers could be. I didn't, I honestly didn't, want to be right about my thoughts, but I knew I'd have to meet with Ben soon and put my ideas and reasons behind them to him, and let him consider it. After all, he's the professional. And all the while I'd be doing that, I'd be wanting to scream at him for keeping me in the dark about his new amore, Anita the Witch.

****

John Haggarty had phoned and left a message asking me to start up the therapy group again that very evening, and at the same time my counselling supervisor, Jack, called within minutes of John's call to see how I was feeling.

"I was thinking of you and the events that are happening around Jacques Station and your area. It seemed like you might be caught up in the middle of all this and might want to spend some time talking about everything," Jack said as soon as I answered the phone.

Jack was right—I did need a shoulder to cry on. But his was not the one I was hoping for.

And if the right shoulder, Ben's, turned up in the next few hours, I would possibly consider doing him serious harm for not keeping me abreast of what had been happening in his love life.

Not that that was anything to do with me, except that common courtesy would suggest that he let me know about his plans. And maybe I'd nudge him to get the divorce finalized.

It would only take a few seconds of his time to sign those papers, and we'd no longer be man and wife.

I sniffed back tears, told myself to grow up and get on with my own life. I should wish Ben well with his new relationship, and act like a grownup. Really, I should.

I picked up my cell phone and was about to dial when the phone rang in my hand. It was a former client of mine, Lucy Blake, Lady Lavinia Blake's daughter, who was calling. She asked if I could find the time to see her the next day.

She is a highly strung young woman who has had a lot to cope with—mainly, a domineering and overbearing mother—and I agreed that I could see her the next afternoon.

I called John Haggarty back and said I would show up for the counselling session at the halfway house, same time, same place. John sounded pleased that I didn't want to pull out after the trouble that had blown up in the group, so I wrote the note down in my diary and got ready to face the world.

Chapter Sixteen

For the rest of the afternoon, I found it difficult to take my mind off Ben and his new love. It was all the more puzzling when Ben hadn't mentioned anything to me about Anita. Not even a passing, "By the way, Gracie, I'm thinking of getting married again to my new love."

Somehow, the hurt I felt was lit up by a stab of anger. How could he let that woman spring a surprise like that on me?

And I really didn't care if he was in love with her. At least, that's what I told myself as I prowled around my living room. He was entitled to that—we hadn't been together for a long time. It was just the cold-blooded way he let Anita dump the news on me instead of being man enough to tell me himself that hurt. Really.

Anyhow, evening was coming, the clocks had gone back an hour from Daylight Savings Time, and I had no time to wallow. It was time for this girl to get to work, trying to fathom out the problems and hopes that could be worked through to keep that bunch of male predators on the straight and narrow when they were finally fully released.

The drive from Jacques Station to Kingston this evening seemed longer than usual, partly because the roads were gleaming with frost and, in some areas, an inch or more of snow had settled. The sky, a foreboding gunmetal blue as it faded into evening, was giving fair warning of snow to come.

As well, I was uncomfortably aware of the dangerous driving in my wild dash towards the woods the other day, when I'd stupidly believed the note left on my car was a lead to finding my daughter, Becky, missing now these past five years. It still hurt that I had fallen so easily into that trap laid by Seth Marshal.

Just thinking of that man, and what he did—and the narrow escape I'd had thanks to my brave friend, the Reverend Allie—made me shiver.

I'd only just had the garage deliver my car back after the repairs it needed following the high-speed skid on a road very like this one, where even with hefty snow tires the road was treacherous.

I'd walked away with a nasty bump on my head and a huge wad of embarrassment after my almost-ex-husband had found me crashed by the side of the country road.

I didn't want to go through that again, so I left home early and took my time driving to the city.

"Gracie—I'm glad you could make it tonight, especially on such short notice," Supervisor John Haggarty greeted me as I entered the halfway house.

"No problem, John. Right now, keeping busy is a good thing." I was glad of the warmth inside the building as I took off my coat and stowed my gloves in the pockets.

"I am so sorry about what happened with Seth. I am sure you're pretty shaken up. I am assuming the police will be pressing charges after he assaulted you? It was a pretty serious matter, and I have agreed that Seth should be taken to prison to await a hearing."

"I'm not sure what is happening, actually—I guess that's going to be in your department to decide, along with the cops, once the truth is known about how Seth got out and found his way to my house in Jacques Station. I suspect there'll be an inquiry. Myself, I'd have the guy sent to the salt mines or somewhere." I tried to add a smile to my comment. I knew how dedicated John was to his work and how harrowing this incident with Seth must have been for him.

"Not as harrowing as it must have been for you, Gracie. I'm glad you feel able to carry on, as the group meetings you take are an asset and I believe are actually doing something to keep some of these guys on the straight and narrow when they leave here.

"As for Seth, he was a problem from the very beginning, but I never thought he'd manage to find a way to leave the house without permission."

"Do you know how that happened? I know you don't usually give anyone permission to leave the house in the evening except under special conditions."

"It's still under investigation, and believe me, there'll be trouble down on the head of whoever was careless enough to allow it." John's normally calm features were flushed with anger.

As it turned out, the men who showed up for the counselling session that evening were subdued and very solicitous for my wellbeing. I was pleased to see Lyle among the ones who sat in the circle. His arm and chest were still bandaged, but he wore his injury like a medal.

And I was touched when he came over to me and held out his hand.

"I wanted to thank you, Dr. Pelham, for your understanding and for coming to see me in the hospital.

I'll never forget your kindness."

His words brought tears to my eyes, and I thought that here was a young man who'd not experienced a lot of kindness in his life. But it seemed that he was now at least more able and confident to stand up for himself. I swiftly shook the young man's hand and started the proceedings.

In fact, as I said to John Haggarty later that evening, it seemed as if the other men had a new respect for the little guy. The result was that Lyle seemed to have a new lease on life, being more interactive in the group and prepared to speak out when he had something to say, with an assurance that caused the others to listen. After watching the interchanges during the session, I felt able to relax with a sense that Lyle, who I once worried was close to suicide, was now an equal member of the group.

John laughed when I stopped in to report on my group session and say goodnight. "It's amazing how these group dynamics work," he said. "The good thing is that I don't believe Lyle has a violent bone in his body—even if he did attack the group bully. I don't see him carrying that behavior further, and if it gives him the guts to stay the course, then that's all good."

I stayed for a welcome cup of invigorating hot coffee and to spend a few minutes with John, planning out our next group meeting and discussing the apparent progress we'd made as well as the occasional worries that lingered following the incident with Seth.

The drive home was uneventful. The snow that had begun on my journey to Kingston seemed to have changed its mind and now the road was slippery but mostly clear and safe if one kept to a reasonable speed.

I have an unfortunate tendency to be impulsive,

something my grandmother had warned me about and my soon-to-be ex-husband had repeatedly criticized as a dangerous character trait.

However, on that late evening drive with the stars peppering the sky and a full moon rising, I felt both at peace and powerful. Passing a signpost to Greenfield Way, I realized I was only minutes away from Vera's home if I took a short side road. *What harm could I possibly do by calling in to see if one of my bereavement group members was all right?* Vera had certainly been very upset when I last saw her, although I knew her fellow group members had comforted her.

I was also hoping to get news of Elsie, who I'd heard nothing from since she left the group meeting under the shadow of the dreaded Sophia.

It took several minutes before Vera, who I knew had suffered the loss of her husband to cancer and then the loss of her son to drugs, came to the door. The outside light flicked on, and she peered at me through the glass and mesh screen door.

"I can't talk right now," Vera said, her voice sounding strained.

"I was just checking in to see if you were all right. I know you were very upset at the last group," I said, speaking as calmly as possible.

Something was wrong. I could see it in Vera's face, and in the tension of her shoulders.

"I'm tired. I really don't want to talk now. I…I probably won't come to group any more—it's all too upsetting," Vera's voice was hoarse as if she'd been crying.

"Are you sure you don't want some company for a little while? And I could murder a cup of tea…"

Something in Vera's face when I said the word "murder"—*How stupid of me!*—signaled that something was very wrong.

But a few minutes later, I had to accept that I was probably one of the last people she wanted to talk to. It was getting late, and we were both tired, so I simply stuck my card in the wire of the screen door and told her she could call or text me at any time if she needed to.

Then I wished her goodnight, but I was troubled as I drove away.

I was even more troubled when I arrived back in my own parking spot in front of my house and saw—well, devastation.

Vomit rose in my throat and tears spilled from my eyes as I took in the horrible scene before me.

The flower boxes that adorned the ground floor windows had been pulled down and the contents scattered, the boxes smashed beyond redemption.

But what made me want to throw up was the series of foul language swear words spray-painted on the pale blue paint of the house's wooden siding.

And on the door, the pièce de resistance, were the words: "Mind Your Own Effing Business, bitch!" Except the word wasn't "effing" but more crude.

I sat in my car and wept to see my grandmother's house defaced in such a manner. Finally, aware that the car was cooling and I was starting to shiver, I took a deep breath and went inside, hoping against hope that the perpetrator had not been able to find access into my home.

I was, I suppose, lucky that whoever did this—and who am I kidding? Of course Sophia's wicked hand was in this somewhere—hadn't been able to get inside the house to continue their desecration of my home. My hand was shaking on my phone when I dialed the local police station and reported the vandalism. I told the officer in charge that I did not think I was in any danger, but that the vandalism was pretty extensive to the house's exterior.

I added that I didn't think it necessary for an officer to come out to my home that evening, as I knew from Ben that they were out once more keeping watch for a murderer. Or murderers. A chill ran down my spine as I thought of Elsie and Vera and the cruel anger that had contaminated them.

"But maybe they could look my place over as part of their nighttime drivebys," I told the desk officer, who agreed that would be a good idea and told me to call in the meantime if I had the faintest sense of anxiety that my intruder might return.

I shivered involuntarily as I put the phone down, and I knew for sure who the murderer—or murderers—were now.

And for the first time in my life, even including Seth's attack on me, I felt unsafe in my own home.

I said a little prayer that my worries were exaggerated. After all, would kind, gentle older ladies like Vera and Elsie really partake in murder? Especially as they were in a group for bereaved mothers…would they be willing to involve themselves in the deaths of other mothers' sons?

The thought was like a heavy weight on my shoulders as I went around my old home's interior, making sure all windows and doors were locked up tightly. Then I poured myself a stiff glass of whisky, a drink I never normally indulge in. The expensive brand had been a gift several Christmases ago from Jack, my supervisor.

Aside from the cheap wine Allie and I indulged in on our Friday night get-togethers, I didn't drink strong liquor normally, but believe me, after the last few days—and especially tonight—I figured I deserved a good glass.

Sleep didn't come easily, as my heart rate responded to every single bump and clatter around the outside of the house. The wind gathered strength, causing tree branches to brush and scratch against the walls like evil fingernails—oh, my, maybe I should cut down on the Halloween horror movies that Allie and I like so much.

Chapter Seventeen

I never have been a "morning person." In fact, if I ruled the world, no one would need to surface from their warm bed until at least nine a.m.

This morning, I offered the excuse that I had only slept fitfully for an hour or so.

Which is why, when my doorbell, my telephone, and my cell phone all started screeching at the same time, along with a painful hammering against my front door, I came awake with a start.

And with violence in my heart.

It's five a.m. Five a.m.! I ask you—who on earth thinks it's okay to set off such a cacophony of noise so early in the morning?

I was sure the very timbers of this century-old home were groaning in sympathy as I dragged myself out of that snug, warm bed.

A glance at my cell phone showed that the one person I know who would be brave enough do this was, well, the one person I know who'd do this. My almost-ex-husband.

I wanted to climb right back into my nest and pull the blankets up to my nose in hopes that he'd go away. At least until the sun was properly risen in the morning sky. Or maybe join me…for a nap! I actually blushed as that thought was quickly pushed from my mind.

But he didn't. And I knew he wouldn't.

And wakefulness brought the full reality of the previous evening's events, and my heart started to pound as I remembered all I'd hoped to forget with a few hours' sleep. I winced as I glanced out the window and took in the view of devastation of my home village left by the awful fire—was it really only a few weeks ago? Shivering as I looked out of my bedroom window, it felt like the shocking event had only just happened. Even though a lot of clean-up work was done, homes that were beyond salvation had been razed to the ground, repairs were being carried out, and new foundations being laid. The memory of that awful night still hurt my heart.

And now we were facing the possibility of some local people taking the law into their own hands to avenge their children…

I blinked back tears as I gathered my energy to go down and see what Ben wanted so early in the morning. I guessed that one of his fellow officers had ratted me out about the call I'd made to the police station about the graffiti and damage to my home.

I grabbed my pink fluffy robe—okay, everyone has their own opinions about ugly pink fluffy bathrobes, and I don't want to hear yours—and made my way slowly down the narrow staircase,

I moved slowly because I was afraid if I rushed to open the door before I quelled the irritation about the early morning wakeup call, I might well attack my almost-ex-husband.

Mind you, the expression on his face as he took in my spiky bedhead hair and, okay, yes, the scruffy pink fluffy robe, did little to mollify me.

Even when he pushed through the door, bringing in the almost arctic morning air, and grabbed me in his arms like I was the most precious creature on the face of the planet.

"Geez, Gracie—I was worried sick! Why for fuck's sake did you not answer the door?"

"Watch your language, Officer. And I didn't answer the door because some sick idiot can't read the clock to know that this is an ungodly hour…"

Ben rolled his eyes. "Listen, Gracie, I haven't been to bed yet. I arrived back in the station to get a message that you'd been in touch and said your home had been attacked and—"

I sniffed. "I'm pretty darn sure I didn't say 'attacked.' I did say that it had been defaced by 'someone' but I didn't need an officer to come by at that time of night. I knew you were all out detecting or whatever it is you're doing, and I was exhausted and just wanted to sleep."

And then I thought again of the horrible graffiti and the shattered planters on the front of my house and burst into tears.

Ben groaned. "Oh, Gracie, what am I going to do with you?" And then he took me in his arms, whispering quiet comfort as I let myself mourn the events of the past few days. It felt so right, being held by him, the way our bodies molded together, the male scent of him, the sheer rightness of our being together. And I cried some more for all that had divided us.

****

I'd just got Ben settled with a big mug of coffee and left him to start frying some bacon and eggs in my big, old-fashioned kitchen. I was on my way to get dressed and was thinking longingly of a hot shower when my cell pinged with a text from Vera.

As I went to open that text, I noticed there was a previous one from her that read: *Couldn't talk to u last night. Sophia was here. Wanted to know where you lived. I told her. Sorry. Vera*

I slumped down on the bench in the hallway, my head resting against the coats on the rack above. That's so great. Really great. Now that crazy woman knows where I live.

It took a moment to hit me. I'm a bit slow before my first coffee. The only reason Sophia wanted my home address was to come and wreak havoc. When I wasn't home, she decided to take her wrath out on my poor old house, wrecking the planters and writing horrible things on the innocent blue wooden siding. I groaned.

Ben must have heard me, because he came out of the kitchen clutching a thick bacon-on-toast sandwich. How had he made it so quickly? Silently I handed him my phone to read the text, and his face turned thunderous.

"Who is this Sophia?" he demanded.

My stomach hurt. I felt like I was going to throw up. The scent of the bacon sandwich didn't improve my guts. I reluctantly knew I had to tell Ben about my suspicions about Sophia. What else could I do?

We went back into the kitchen, and I sat at the round, pretty table while Ben poured us both coffees. He handed me one of the mugs and stood looking at me, waiting to hear the story.

"I was planning to discuss this with you today when you dropped by. That was before I saw what had been done to my house. Sophia…I think Sophia is…no, wait. You said there were three daggers used in the murders?"

"That's true. But the lab only found one set of fingerprints on all three weapons."

"Which means only one person was the actual killer?" I held my breath, afraid to get the answer.

"That's how it looks, right now. Now, for the love of all that's sane, will you please tell me what you think you know?"

Suddenly I felt like I'd got a reprieve. If there was only one set of fingerprints on those daggers, then only one person was doing the killing...maybe Elsie and Vera were in the clear.

"You know I work with a bereaved mothers' group, and most of the women who attend have lost their sons or daughters to drugs...right?"

Ben nodded, taking a huge bite out of his sandwich.

"Well, Sophia was new to our group, which is usually a calm, sad event, hearing a new person's story, and people try to help each other get through the grief—if that's at all possible."

I could almost hear Ben's teeth grinding as he waited for me to finish my story.

"Anyhow, Sophia made it plain that she didn't think enough was being done to stop the drug dealers...and that something a little more drastic..."

And then the doorbell rang.

They say it never rains but it pours. Well, it looks like real life was intent on dropping an absolute, freaking deluge on my head.

When I answered, Jack, my supervisor, was standing on the doorstep, clutching one of those pretty bouquets from the gas station on Highway Seven. I have often thought Jack had a bit of a crush on me, but I can say without hesitation that, viewing me in my bedhead hair and pink fluffy bathrobe probably exploded all his fantasies in two seconds.

Jack came in, bringing with him a shroud of cold air. "I was worried about you, Gracie. I called yesterday but you didn't get back to me. Is everything all right?"

I really didn't know how to answer that. I would have thought that having seen the awful mess around my front door he'd have figured out for himself that everything was definitely not all right.

But that's Jack for you.

****

I sipped a cup of life-giving coffee and scanned my emails as I left Jack and Ben glaring at each other over the bouquet of flowers. As I climbed the stairs, I found an email from Vera: "*Couldn't talk last night, Sophia had just come into my house and was talking like a deranged person. I was seriously a bit afraid, and it was a relief when she left. I don't know where she went. She was angry. I talked to Elsie this morning, and we want to come to your house and give ourselves up to that cop if you can be there to see it's all proper.*"

I hadn't time to get properly dressed and had just put the two men in the kitchen with instructions to stay there until I gave them the all-clear. I needed to find out what the two women wanted before I set Detective Dog—i.e., my almost-ex—onto them.

Vera and Elsie arrived soon after, looking pale but determined. I didn't miss the raised-eyebrow looks they gave me and my pink fluffy housecoat. It's better not to try to explain some things.

Well, I decided it would be better if I could speak to them before they were left to Ben's cop mercy. I quickly poured two cups of tea and herded the two women through the house, past my office, and into the small glassed-in porch at the back of the house.

"I'd like you to stay right here until I come to get you. If necessary, lock the door. I need to talk to you before the police do—we need to work out your story."

Elsie and Vera nodded in unison, reminding me of those circus dolls that used to be displayed in glass boxes at fairgrounds. I gave one last warning to stay put or else, and left the room.

As I closed the door, I heard one of them exclaim, "Did you see what she was wearing? That pink fluffy thing at this time of the day?"

"Maybe her ex-husband gets a thrill out of it. Wasn't that handsome hunk who was in the kitchen her ex, the cop?"

"I don t know—there were two handsome hunks in the kitchen. Neither looked very happy."

Muffled laughter followed me down the corridor.

I tamed the desire to go back and give them a piece of my mind—after all, they were part of the reason I was in this mess! But the siren calls of a hot shower trumped the need to sanction my guests.

I again left Jack and Ben still glaring at each other from opposite sides of my kitchen table and made a hasty retreat to my upstairs ensuite. No way was I dealing with any of this without a warm shower and a change of clothes.

It's hard to be taken seriously when you're wearing a flimsy cotton nightdress and a pink fluffy bathrobe.

And I had a very real feeling that there was serious stuff that was going to need some expert sorting. Just the sort of thing a psychology counsellor is trained to do.

Chapter Eighteen

When I emerged from my upstairs sanctuary, clean and dressed in more conventional working attire, I was shocked to find that the deluge of people in my house had expanded beyond belief. I wondered if I could possibly slip out of the house and book myself a ticket on some exotic cruise, travelling somewhere from whence I would return, suntanned and relaxed, to find that all this kerfuffle was solved and my home was once more peaceful.

Won't happen! a miserable little voice in my head declared, and I had to admit there was no chance of escape for me.

Above the growing number of voices, I heard a gentle tapping on the front door. I couldn't ignore it, so I opened it to find Millie and her cat standing on my doorstep, looking lost. I had to lean down to hear her tiny voice.

"I'm sorry to bother you, Gracie. But my electricity has gone off, and it's very cold in my house. I wouldn't ask for help if it was just me, but you know how Maxie feels the cold…" The moth-eaten old tomcat peered out at me from a ratty looking blanket, his green eyes huge.

Millie's voice trailed off sadly. This was a lady who had lived alone most of her life and survived as well as she could without imposing on anyone. And now her electric heaters had gone off, and she was upset because her cat was cold. Tears sprang to my eyes.

"Millie, you just come inside and get yourself and Maxie warm, and I'll get one of those lazy men to go over to your house and see what's happening. Do you have a key they could use?"

Millie gave a watery smile as she fumbled into her housecoat pocket. She produced a key which had a little red ribbon attached to it. Handing it over to me, she said shyly: "I have different colored ribbons on all my keys, so I know which one is which."

"That's very organized of you," I said. "Now, you go into my kitchen and get a hot cup of tea. There's some leftover chicken bits in the fridge if you think Maxie would like them. Then find yourself a comfy seat, and we'll see if we can make the men useful."

Millie gave a grateful smile and trotted off into the kitchen to get herself a drink—but I knew she'd find some food for Maxie before seeing to herself. I followed her into the kitchen and surveyed the two men sitting on opposite sides of my table.

"Okay, one of you, I need someone who knows about electric heaters," I announced.

Both Jack and Ben immediately jumped up, each obviously prepared to be my knight in shining white armor.

"Now, Ben, I need you here to talk to Vera and Elsie about murdering drug pushers, a bad habit they need to stop," I said, pleased at the flush that pinked Jack's cheeks. Ben was a bit more used to my strange sense of humor. "So, Jack, it looks like you're up. Here's Millie's housekey, the house across the road—her hydro has gone off, and she needs some help getting the heat back."

I dispatched Jack towards the front door, the red-ribboned door key clutched in his hand as I told him he was a savior for poor Miss Millie and her cat.

Just then I heard a familiar voice in my hallway and dashed out to welcome my best friend, the Reverend Allie. If Allie was here, then we'd get a lot of these people sorted out.

I hugged my friend. "I knew I could rely on you, but how did you know I needed you?" I asked.

"Well, you know what villages are like! I heard so many stories about the goings-on here today—and last night—that I just had to come and see what you were actually up to. And I brought a bottle of white wine to stock your refrigerator."

"Honey, I could just stick a straw in that bottle and slurp it up!" I told her.

"So, tell me what's happening."

I led her into the parlor, which was thankfully free of surplus people right now, and gave her first the list— the graffiti on my house frontage, the lack of electricity in Millie's home, the competitive looks between Ben and Jack, and the elderly ladies who were probably going to face some kind of punishment for trying to kill drug dealers.

I didn't know whether to be offended or just irritated as she held her sides laughing, with tears running down her cheeks.

"Oh, Gracie!" she managed to gasp out. "I don't know anyone who can get into so much trouble—and such unusual trouble—as you! And you don't even try, do you? The trouble finds you."

I glared at her but couldn't keep up the nasty grimace for long and soon I was laughing, too. After all, she was right. I didn't know anyone who got into the kind of difficulties I did, and all the while I was actually meaning well.

Finally, Allie collapsed onto the couch and cleared her throat. "So, tell me more about what or who you're dealing with here, and let's see if we can sort it out and save you from further mischief."

I tried to explain about Sophia, the woman from my bereaved mothers' group, and how angry she seemed to be with me, for some reason, and the others she was influencing who might be involved with her in trying to get revenge on the drug pushers they considered responsible for the deaths of some of the young people in the area. That, at least, sobered Allie up for a few minutes.

Then I told her, in a low murmur, about the arrival of Jack, my suspicions that he carried a torch for me, and the way he and Ben had sat glaring at each other in my kitchen like sworn enemies.

I could see my friend was trying hard to suppress her giggles, and I was trying to keep a straight face myself.

After mentioning Millie, who was currently enjoying a cup of tea in my kitchen, I explained more about the two retired ladies sitting in my sun porch, awaiting their fateful meeting with Detective Ben Pelham.

"The poor things must be terrified," I told Allie.

But my friend wasn't sympathetic. "You'd think they would know better at their age than to go out and about with someone who is obviously not quite right in the head. Did they think this Sophia woman would just produce a leather strap and give the bad guys a good slap across the bottom, like they used to do in schools before corporal punishment was banned?" Allie said.

I was stuck for words. I didn't know just how deep Elsie and Vera were into these terrible murders. I prayed silently that they'd only been on the periphery, as I couldn't in a million years understand what had driven those two reputable ladies into the equivalent of blood lust.

"I think they thought this was just some sort of scare tactic, that the guys dealing drugs would be cowed and rush off home to their mommies and ask forgiveness.

"But the truth is, these guys were convinced they were safe and could set about making a pile of money ruining other people's kids' lives. They thought they were too smart for any kind of retribution.

"And the really scary, sickening thing is that Sophia, the ringleader, got herself armed with three horrible, sharp daggers…one for each of the three of them. I think it was seeing those daggers that brought the reality home to Elsie and Vera of how wrong this all was going—as well as the knowledge that someone—I suspect it must have been Sophia—actually murdered the three young men."

Allie wasn't laughing any more. "Dear Lord above, Gracie—how did all this happen in our little village? Why did no one notice? We're still in shock over the horrendous fire, still trying to get our heads around what the future for us may hold, and yet these women decided to take the law into their own hands?"

I agreed it was hard to understand. "I think there are two things—the first is that these are two mothers who have lost children in a horrible way to drugs, and secondly, I don't think they actually understood that Sophia was prepared to kill—apparently already had killed—and expected them to be willing to do the same."

Allie was silent for a few moments. "Well, I can only say thank you to the Lord that they somehow saw the light."

"Well, Ben and I will talk to Vera and Elsie. I want to be sure they understand he's a cop and they're, well, they're in trouble. And then I hope Jack manages to get Millie's heat fixed, and she and her cat can go home—remind me to get some stuff out of my freezer for her. And then we should…"

My thoughts were interrupted by a loud knock at my door. The trepidation I felt at the prospect of another visitor must have shown on my face, because Allie got up. "I'll get the door, and I'll see Millie and her cat home once we hear that the guy you sent over there has fixed it. If he hasn't fixed it, well, Millie and her cat can come and stay at the manse until we get it sorted. Certainly, we won't let her be cold and hungry with her cat…"

The front door was pushed open, and I went to see who the latest visitor was. Turned out it was the reeve and several of the village council workmen, all standing staring at the graffiti on the front of my house.

"I hope we're not interfering, Gracie. Looks like you have a house full, but we know how much you love this old house, how you keep it looking so good. In fact, your house is the first one anyone coming into the village sees, and so it gives a really good impression of Jacques Station…and Lord knows, it needs all the help we can get, what with the fire damage… So the guys and I, we thought we'd come along and clean up the front of your house. Sam and Alan are pretty good carpenters, and they're going to rebuild the plant boxes. In the meantime, Alex, Bob, and I are going to clean that awful fecking mess off the front… I hope you don't think we're interfering…"

Tears filled my eyes. The people are the reason I love this village so much! "That is really wonderful of you! I can't thank you enough. And there's paint left over from the last time we painted the siding. It's all down in the back room, in a cupboard past the washer and dryer…"

"Okay, lads, let's get to work…"

And within minutes there seemed to be a blur of activity as my grandmother's house got a facelift. I brushed away tears of gratitude and went back inside, knowing the guys were experienced and would do a good job.

Chapter Nineteen

So, with my house being prettied up back to its grand self, and Jack busy in Millie's house doing something useful, I paused to check on Ben, who was lurking in the kitchen and probably overdosing on coffee as he waited to see Elsie and Vera.

Call me cruel, but I had to smother a laugh as I peered in to see Ben looking somewhat pale as Mrs. LeBlanc advanced on him.

Mrs. LeBlanc is my sixty-ish client who has decided she missed out on the sexual revolution and so deserves to catch up on all she missed as a teenager. She was brought up very strictly, married off by her parents when she was very young, and believes she missed out on a lot of fun. She's now determined to catch up, much to the horror of her straitlaced son—who, by the way, is paying for her sessions with me.

I hadn't heard her come in, but now I saw she'd got Ben pinned by the refrigerator as she regaled him with a somewhat salacious-sounding story about her good-looking teenaged gardener. Millie was an avid audience.

What Ben didn't know was that most of Mrs. LeBlanc's sexual fantasies were, in fact, entirely fantasy. That's what we'd been working on in her sessions with me.

I thought it would be kind to rescue him, and I explained to Mrs. LeBlanc that we needed to postpone our session until the next day, as things were a little crazy around here right now.

"Well, I was just telling this nice gentleman here…"

"No, Mrs. LeBlanc, this nice gentleman is a senior police officer who really needs to get back to work." I gave Ben a surreptitious wink as I spoke.

With a deep sigh, Mrs. LeBlanc threw Ben one last air kiss and slowly moved away.

When she was gone from the room, I guessed it was time to get him together with Vera and Elsie.

"I don't want to repeat everything they told me, as I think it's best for you to hear their story yourself directly from them," I said. But first I warned him that the two women were fragile after the stress they had been under.

"I'll be gentle," he replied, with a slight smile on his lips.

I was very worried about the outcome of this. I could feel an anxiety headache starting to pound in my temples as I considered the worst possible scenario—that the two women would face criminal charges. I had no idea how deeply they were embroiled in this whole issue of Sophia and her attempts to destroy the drug trade by killing youthful drug dealers, but my stomach roiled as I imagined the two older ladies in jail outfits…

Having anything at all to do with a potential violent act, not to mention possible murder, was something the courts tended to frown upon.

Will my two friends find themselves doing jail time? At their age?

Just how deep have these two women allowed themselves to be pulled into Sophia's madness?

Then I thought of Sophia, wondering how much she had been pushed to a breaking point, one where she considered murdering young men to be a justified action. Just what was the story behind her behavior? Then my stomach roiled at the idea that Sophie had been able to lure the other women into almost carrying out such a terrible deed. I was so grateful that their inner decency had stopped them going further, but I also knew from Ben that it was quite likely Sophia had murdered at least three young men—probably four—in her crusade to stop the drug dealing.

As we headed to the sunroom, I broached the subject of the possible penalties Vera and Elsie might face, but Ben said it wasn't possible to second guess what might happen until he and his fellow officers had all the facts.

"Vera and Elsie have something on their consciences, and they want to talk to you," I told him. "I wanted to talk to you earlier, but I have been very worried the two of them went along with something terrible."

Something maybe involving daggers.

"But when you said there was only one set of fingerprints on those daggers that had been used to kill that poor…"

Ben made an irritated sighing sound. "Gracie, Gracie… I can't do anything until I hear what these two ladies want to talk about. You said they wanted to confess…?"

I nodded, reduced to chewing my bottom lip in exasperation and anxiety.

"Well, I think I had better meet them, and then we'll go from there."

Does he mean pass "confess" and go straight to jail?

My stomach was knotted with anxiety as I led the

way to the little glassed-in porch. It was no doubt getting cold in there, and I wasn't sure I'd turned on the heater…

So it was with some trepidation that I led him into the bright room with its view over my grandmother's flower garden. Not that the view would be there for long, as snow was imminent, daylight savings time was already gone, and the days were an hour less in daylight than they had been just days ago.

Elsie and Vera were still sitting on the wicker chairs, exactly where I'd left them, although I was glad one of them had thought to turn on the heater.

"Ladies, this is Ben Pelham. As you know, he's a detective who has been following up on these… incidents…" I swallowed back on the word "murders." "He's the best person to speak to about the issues that are bothering you."

Vera was sniffing back tears, but Elsie sat up straight in her chair and looked Ben right in the eye as she took a deep breath and began her story.

With an occasional nudge from Vera, she told of how they belonged to the bereaved group, and how they'd moved emotionally from sadness to anger as they listened to the woman named Sophia alternatively berate them for their passive behavior and coax them into the idea that they should do something about the growing drug problem.

"It made sense, because it seemed that no one else, not even you guys in the police, were doing anything to protect our village children from the dealers," Vera cut in. "It seemed like a way that we could be, like, vigilantes, to watch in the evenings and give those young guys selling drugs a good telling off so they'd back off."

"But in God's truth, we neither of us meant to…to

hurt or kill a young one…we just wanted to give them a bit of a scare…and then we saw the daggers, and all of a sudden, we knew what was going to happen…"

"So why did you not approach the police with what you knew?" Ben asked, frowning.

The two women were silent for a few moments.

"I think you can say that we were both very afraid, not of what we'd done, but of what we thought we were going to do if we followed Sophie's lead." Vera said, her face going paler.

"You see, we never knew that Sophie had actually killed someone…not until two nights ago, when we went out with her…" Elsie added in a tiny voice.

Ben frowned. "Ladies, if what you are saying is correct, then this Sophia could be the person of interest we need to talk to, quite possibly responsible for several deaths, and she seriously needs to be stopped."

By this time both women were crying, and I had to resist going over to them and hugging them both. I did hand them the box of tissues that I'd left on the side table, and both women nodded their thanks.

There was a communal sniffing, nose blowing, and wiping of eyes as Vera and Elsie struggled to regain their composure.

There was no way I could imagine either of them doing harm to anyone…

"We know we have some responsibility because we didn't do anything to stop Sophia. When we realized that this wasn't just a bit of fun, maybe a chance to feel like we were in charge of something, we could have maybe tried to stop her…but we honestly didn't want to believe…that Sophia had actually killed someone. Or wanted us to take part…"

There was a moment's silence, and I could almost hear the tears.

"Not until we saw the blood on the daggers when Sophia came around to Vera's house. We'd just been talking about what we were going to do about everything when Sophia arrived and...and she was quite proud to show us the blood..."

"So that's why you didn't want to talk to me when I stopped at your home, Vera?" I saw the whole thing now.

"That's right. Sophia has taken a real dislike to you. She says you're part of the reason nothing has been done because you're too chicken-hearted and always going on about feelings, and being too soft while our children die..." Vera said.

I felt her words like a dagger to my own heart. Had I been wrong to tell these women they should be gentle with themselves and others and try to come to terms with their losses?

As if they read my mind, Vera took my hands and said, "Don't feel bad, Gracie. Your way of coping was far better than Sophia's. I don't think I could live with myself if I'd killed some young boy."

"It's true, Gracie. We'd have been no better than the drug pushers who were responsible for our children's deaths, if we'd killed one of them." Elsie gave me a watery smile. "After all, those boys also had mothers who probably loved them."

Ben stood up and stretched. "Ladies, I have to take you to the police station, and there'll be a lot of questions needing answers. At this point I can't see that you have actually committed a crime, other than withholding evidence that could have taken a very dangerous woman off the streets before she could find another victim.

Another mother's son," he added, seeing the way both women winced.

"Will we go to prison?" Vera asked, her voice trembling.

"That, I am afraid, is a matter for the police and the courts to decide. I would advise that you each call for a lawyer, or one will be provided for you if you cannot afford to hire one."

Ben added, "I also have to tell you that a fourth young man was stabbed to death last night." His statement sent shock waves through all three of us. Elsie and Vera looked so pale I was afraid they would collapse or have heart attacks.

After he called for police transportation for the two women, Ben sat with them, waiting, until reinforcements arrived. He had put out a BOLO—an all-points bulletin for all officers to be on the lookout for Sophia, along with her description, car make, and whatever other details he'd been able to find out.

"I'm going to make tea," I said, that being the only thing of comfort I was able to think up as I looked at the pale but now composed faces of the two women.

I asked Reverend Allie to come and sit with them, also, and offer whatever comfort she could. Seeing how shaken they were, I asked Ben to be sure to have a doctor on hand at the station when the two women were questioned.

I knew these were good women, driven by grief to try to atone for the deaths of their children. In my mind I cursed the drug dealers and the woman who had decided to take the law into her own hands and drag these two into the mess with her.

Chapter Twenty

Jack came back looking like he'd been investigating the bowels of the earth—and, he explained, his experience was pretty much in that line.

He pulled a dusty spiderweb off his jacket, shuddered as he looked at it, and then managed to unstick it from his fingers and put it in the garbage.

Allie and I, meanwhile, were busy trying not to laugh at his disheveled state—not at all like the well-groomed gentleman who'd arrived at my home just a couple of hours ago.

"Stop laughing," he growled. "I've been down in the basement at Millie's home. It's a good thing I'm not allergic to cats, because there must be twenty of all shapes and sizes running around in a penned-off area down there." He sniffed and made a martyred expression that fooled no one. "Well, that might have been a slight exaggeration, but there were three or four kittens…and an aggressive mommy cat who made it plain she'd rip my throat out if I got near her babies."

"Oh, dear." Allie sighed. "It sounds like Millie is collecting cats again. We'll have to call the Humane Society and hope they can house them."

"Did you manage to fix the heating?" I asked, crossing my fingers.

He perked up considerably. "I used to work in the building trade—pay was good and paid my university fees and more. So I learned quite a bit about heating and general home care." He gratefully accepted a cup of hot coffee from Allie, added a heaping spoonful of sugar, and dosed it with cream. "In the end, the problem was simple to solve—somehow a breaker had blown in the hydro panel."

Allie and I put on expressions of admiration.

"How did you know where to look?" I asked.

"The panel is in the basement, along with all those litter boxes and kittens…and about a million spiders and their webs. The basement is split into two, and the wall with the breaker box is in the second half, at the far end of the basement. Doesn't the woman ever go down there?"

I smiled admiringly. "I doubt she even knows about the hydro box or anything about breakers," I told him. "I certainly didn't know she was collecting cats again. We're going to have to find homes for them…" Jack flinched and shook his head decisively.

"Okay, so Jack's not a fan of cats. But if we can't find homes, then we'll have to call in the Humane Society. The cats need to be fixed or there'll be hordes of them all over the village."

Jack took himself to the bathroom and came out some time later with his hands and face spotless again, and his clothes dust-and-spiderweb-free. He then visited the kitchen and told Millie her heating was again working, and he ushered her to the door and across the street as though she were the Queen.

When he returned, I said, "I have to say, Jack, that you did a great job. I don't think Millie could have afforded to bring in an electrician. She'd probably have frozen to death without the heaters." Jack preened a little and then, to my surprise, told me to give him a call if Millie needed anything fixed. "She seems a sweet old lady, aside from the cats, with a very interesting background. Did you know she worked on luxury cruise lines and travelled all over the world, once upon a time?"

Allie and I both looked surprised.

"It's terrible how we take old people for granted," Allie commented. "Who'd have thought she was once on the crew of a luxury liner?"

After a second cup of coffee, Jack turned down an offer of joining us in a pizza delivery and bade us goodbye.

And to my surprise, before he left, he asked if it would be okay for him to take one of the kittens. "It's a feisty little guy, and, well, he needs a proper home and good food," Jack said sheepishly.

"Just speak to Millie first, but I'm sure you can take as many kittens as you like…"

Jack pulled on his jacket and winter boots. He looked at me and smiled. "It's been interesting, Gracie, as it always is with you."

"I hope you mean interesting in a good way, not in a 'Heaven have mercy on me' way?'" I teased.

He smiled, dropped a kiss on my cheek, and was gone.

Allie said she had to go, too, but she would pick up pizza from the little restaurant that was now operating again after the fire and return later after she was finished with some church duties.

I accompanied her to the door and was surprised to see that Reeve Alex McGeary and his men had finished touching up the house paintwork so the horrible words were no longer visible. They'd also repaired the flower boxes and window boxes.

"It's too late in the season to plant anything in there now," he said. "But they'll be good and sturdy when spring comes along."

"Honestly, I can't thank you and the guys enough. I was heartbroken at the mess when I came home the other night and saw what had been done."

I didn't mention the searing pain I had felt that someone would deface my home so crudely. I knew from the sympathetic looks that these guys felt for me.

Reeve McGeary grinned. "At your service, ma'am. Don't hesitate to call if you need anything, or if you're bothered again by the person who did this." And then they were gone.

Chapter Twenty-One

The house seemed suddenly very quiet once everyone had gone about their business.

Millie had gone home with a selection of meals from my freezer, Allie was off to carry out church duties, and Jack was on his way home with two kittens—he said they were brothers and he couldn't bear to separate them. Ben was at the police station with Vera and Elsie, and the big house was so peaceful and quiet.

I sighed with pleasure as I kicked off my shoes and put my feet up on a soft-cushioned footstool. I had a hot cup of coffee, with lots of cream and sugar, at the arm of my chair, a notebook and pen at my elbow in case any great ideas came my way, and the latest bestseller by Canadian writer Louise Penny on my lap.

Can life get any better than this?

Ben had given me an alarm to press which would— at least in theory—sound the alarm in the police station and in nearby police cars. I found great comfort in that. But I was more comforted by the idea that there were several big, strong cops and very smart WPCs around the area, all keeping watch.

By the time I reached chapter two, my coffee was all gone, and I was feeling sleepy after the disturbed rest of the past night, along with all the anxieties of the day.

I went into the kitchen, where the coffeepot was still hot and I refilled my mug. As I poured, I remembered I'd left that alarm on the arm of my chair. Ben would lecture me endlessly if he thought I wasn't carrying the little electronic device around with me, after the lecture he'd given me about keeping myself safe and in touch with the officers in the area. Feeling suddenly vulnerable, I hurried back to pick it up and put it into the pocket of my sweater.

Outside there'd been snow, just enough to have the garden turn into a minor winter wonderland, to use a hackneyed phrase, but not yet deep enough to form drifts. I briefly considered slipping on my boots and parka and taking a stroll around the yard, but common sense—and laziness—prevailed and I returned to my cozy chair in the warm living room.

I realized I was looking forward to Ben returning, hopefully with encouraging news about Vera and Elsie's status. Maybe we would have some time to talk quietly and calmly about our own status, together. I couldn't help but wonder about Anita and her claims that Ben was about to marry her. *Surely, if Ben is about to get married, he'd have mentioned it to me? It would have been the polite thing to do…*

The sun's last hurrah was shining crimson and gold through the living room window as it slowly sank beneath the skyline, and I was nodding off to sleep in the peaceful room.

I should have known it wouldn't last.

The doorbell shrilled in that way doorbells have, the way you know the person ringing them is not going to just give up and go away, no matter how much you might want them to. Whoever had their finger on that button was serious about being noticed.

Maybe, just maybe, if I waited a few moments, this

annoying interrupter would go away. Then I thought, Maybe it's Ben coming back to let me know how everything went with Vera and Elsie. He doesn't have a key to my house...

Or perhaps Allie had picked up the promised wine and pizza and was balancing them in her arms while she pressed the buzzer...although Allie did have a key...

The bell shrilled again, the message loud and clear that whoever was pressing the buzzer wasn't intending to go away.

Oh, hell, I'd better go and see what it's all about...

With the coffee cup in hand, I opened the door, then stepped back in surprise as I saw the stoop was empty. And there was no sign of anyone in the street.

Puzzled and not a little annoyed, I muttered curses under my breath on the heads of some of the less likeable local kids who liked to do things like ring doorbells and run away. I shut the door with a slam and turned to go back—and my heart seemed to stand still as the breath left my body.

The outside door in the kitchen was wide open—I knew I'd left it closed—and standing right there, face wreathed in a nasty smile, was Sophia. The expression on her face made my blood run cold. I had never seen such hatred on a human face—and especially not on the face of someone who barely knew me. *How did such a brief encounter credit such hatred?*

And it was hatred. It gleamed in her eyes and was demonstrated in the tightness of her mouth, in the set of her shoulders.

And clutched in her hands was a sickeningly sharp-looking dagger... Seeing me flinch, she let the manic smile on her face spread evilly. *Sophia is certainly looking like she wants to use that blade. On me!*

This woman didn't just want to frighten me. She didn't just want to kill me. She wanted to plunge that dagger right into my heart and enjoy the act. And maybe try to drag out the pleasure…and my pain.

I gasped her name, which made her evil smile even wider. I was pretty much struggling to keep a calm expression while my heart was thundering in my chest. Too late, I remembered the alarm button that Ben had insisted I should have…

"Sophia—I didn't expect to see you here today. How did you get in?" As I spoke, I remembered the gadget was in my sweater pocket but probably unreachable without signaling to Sophia what I was doing.

Ben had warned me to keep it within easy reach, preferably in my hand, at all times. He was going to be ever so mad at me if he found me stabbed to death because I disobeyed his orders…

Sophia's smile grew wider. "I'm afraid I broke the window in your back door, made a bit of a mess, but that's the least of your worries right now…" And she advanced towards me, the dagger held firmly in her hand and her intention written boldly on her face. "Keep your hands where I can see them!"

The best I could do was press my elbow against my pocket and hope that was sufficient to set the alarm off.

"Sophia, I know we have had our differences, but I think you need some help. Why don't we go into my office, and sit down with a coffee and talk about what's wrong?"

From the expression on the woman's face, I couldn't have said anything more stupid.

I realized at that moment that the woman wasn't just misguided—she was evil. Or insane. As a psychologist, I have never really believed in anyone being evil. Mostly, behavior in my world is put down to some character flaw, maybe a bad experience in childhood, or an inability to feel comfortable in the world...

One look at the sickening grin on Sophie's face, the wild look of excited anticipation in her eyes, and my heart started to hammer even faster. She was insanely excited at the idea of using that shining sharp dagger on me, and I knew then that mentally ill or just plain bad didn't fully describe the woman. In my own practice, I don't recall ever coming across a case as bad as this.

She was evil. She knew she had the upper hand, and she held the dagger as if it were a sensual object, and in that moment, I knew I had to act—or die.

Because she was very obviously enjoying the bloody revenge she was sure was to be hers.

And that revenge was to see my blood running from my body as she brought her dagger down once, twice, three times.

Just as she had done to those three—probably four—young men she had murdered. Ben said they knew of four for sure now. How many more were there?

I struggled to hold back the horrible sense of hysteria that rose in my chest. This woman intended to bring about my death—and I wasn't sure I was strong enough to fight her. After all, she had the advantage of being a crazy bitch...

Then there was no more time to think as Sophia launched herself at me, her eyes wild and her look crazy. They say that crazy people are made extra strong by their craziness...and in that moment, I knew it was true.

Sophia had a strength I couldn't fight.

I backed away as she jumped towards me, hoping she'd give me an advantage by losing her balance. I did a quick inventory of the possible ways I could flee from the house, but the nearest was the front door, at the end of the hallway and beckoning but too far from my reach. Sophia would easily take me down before I got anywhere near that big front door.

Then, as she charged me, I remembered the large cup of coffee in my hand, and I swung it like a matador…temporarily blinding the other woman. Even so, she swiped blindly with the dagger and opened up a long cut on my arm before I was able to dash pash her to the door as she struggled to clear hot liquid from her head and eyes.

I just yanked the door open and fell through it, right into Ben's arms.

It took him just one look at me, the blood seeping through my shirtsleeve, and at the crazy woman down the hallway, and he knew what was happening. He set me to one side and, drawing his weapon, he moved towards the kitchen, but Sophia was gone.

"Dear Lord, you're bleeding!" Ben exclaimed, returning to me. He was already on his radio asking for an ambulance and for assistance in finding and capturing Sophia.

My shoulder was burning, and when I looked, there was a steady trickle of blood going down my arm and onto the scatter rug. In my fear, I hadn't even noticed how long and deep the slash wound was. All I could do was mutter a prayer of thanks that this wound was all I'd suffered.

"Damn, that's going to ruin that pretty rug," I

declared. And then the room started to go dark, and I fell into Ben's arms.

Everything that happened after that was a blur. It seemed unreal—the influx of uniformed officers wearing full protective gear, the arrival of the ambulance, and the sweet way Allie insisted on travelling to the hospital with me, the gathering of neighbors expressing concern and good wishes as I tried to refuse to leave.

"You need to go to the hospital," Allie said firmly. "Let Ben and his officers deal with Sophia, but he doesn't need to be worrying about what's happening to you—you'll be in good hands."

****

I don't remember much of what happened after that, other than a doctor telling me I was lucky the wound wasn't deeper…

"But it was just a nick in my shoulder," I protested.

He gave me a strange look. "It might have been a nick in your shoulder, Dr. Pelham…but it went deep. Any further over on your shoulder and it could have done more serious damage," he said sternly. "Now, lie still while we check the wound again, and the nurse will put on a new dressing."

I was anxious about what was happening with the hunt for Sophia, worried that Ben or one of his men might be ambushed and badly injured—that dagger she carried was big and sharp.

Hours went by without word, even though I used my cell to call the police station, several times, until Allie took the phone away from me and told me I was making a nuisance of myself.

"Let them get on with what they're doing. We don't

want anyone distracted. That could leave them vulnerable to a surprise attack from that woman," Allie said. "Now, get some rest, and if there's any news, I will let you know right away. Trust me?"

I nodded. If I could trust anyone, it was my friend Allie. But I refused to be put into a hospital bed, and instead sat on a hard chair in the waiting room, under the beady eyes of several nurses, and tried not to fall asleep as I waited for news.

Chapter Twenty-Two

The night was long and fraught with anxiety. But finally, in the early morning, Dr. Armand—the same doctor who had examined me after I'd crashed the car—gave me one more checkup and pronounced me fit to return home.

"Now, I'm afraid this is becoming a habit, Dr. Pelham. I mean, the hospital's a lovely place, but you really should be home."

"Maybe she's got a crush on you, Doctor, like so many patients have," one of the nurses said with a sly wink at me. "You wouldn't believe the number of admirers he has!"

I've never seen a doctor blush before, but I have to admit, Dr. Armand is cute...

One of the nurses found an abandoned sweater to cover my bandaged shoulder and arm, and Allie escorted me out to her car.

I flinched when I realized she was driving, and I stepped back away from the car. "Allie, do you think..."

"Oh, give it up, girl. If you can face down a psychotic murdering bitch, you can manage to spend half an hour in the car with me driving. After all, how much worse can that be?" Allie asked.

I'd driven with her before, and I knew just how bad it could be...but I had no other choice. I said a quick prayer for safety, and off we went.

"So, since you've been doing nothing but lying around the hospital, you should know that Tina cleaned up the mess that was left behind at your house, with a little help from your neighbors."

"Wait a minute! Tina helped clean up the mess at my house? Well, that's a first. She didn't booby trap it or anything, did she?"

Allie tried to look stern, but I could see her lips twisting with incipient laughter. "I keep telling you, you really misjudge her. And the reeve came along with some other guys and fixed up that broken window, once the cops gave the all-clear."

I was touched again at the kindness shown by my fellow villagers. "Tina helped to clean up the mess in my house?" I murmured.

Allie gave me a sharp look. "Yes, and Tina sent her best wishes for your recovery. You know, she's not really as horrible as you think. She's just a very insecure person."

I didn't have anything to say to that, so I watched the snowy landscape pass by our windows as we neared home.

I shivered as an idea came into my mind. "What happened with the search for Sophia? Did they find her? Was anyone hurt?"

Allie's expression clouded. She bit her lip, and I knew she was trying to think how to tell me something. Her knuckles showed white as her hands tightened on the steering wheel and she glanced over at me.

"Eyes on the road!" I yelped as a big municipal snowplow came lumbering our way.

"It seems the trail went cold at the Crooked Stream." Allie sighed. "The police think she may have gone into the water. Oh, Gracie, that water is deep with runoff from the snow, and it's freezing cold…"

I shivered at the very idea of that bitter cold water. "Did…was a body found?"

"Not yet. It is possible she made it across the stream and into the woods," Allie told me, but there was doubt in her voice. "I guess time will tell."

We were silent on the rest of the drive. I was longing to get to my home, to step inside the building that feels like a warm cocoon of my grandmother's love. I needed that.

But when Allie pulled up in my driveway, there were several cars there. "Brace yourself, honey," Allie said, a big grin on her face.

The front door opened and a mob of neighbors came spilling out, all smiling and expressing pleasure to see that I was all in one piece.

Small communities leak gossip and information like a sieve. News about my adventures—and near-death experience—had spread throughout the village and out to folks on the side roads. Reeve Alex McGeary gave me a stern look. "This is the second time in just a few days that you have scared the living daylights out of us, Gracie Pelham! What will we do with you?"

My neighbor Millie, clutching that big old tomcat of hers, added mischievously, "We're going to have to get you a bodyguard—kind of like that handsome man over there!"

I looked to where she was pointing and saw Ben, my almost-ex-husband, standing not far away, a big smile on his face. He came over and gently led me inside the house, but I stopped just a few feet inside.

My home was filled with flowers and homemade

food that smelled delicious. Over the kitchen door was a sparkly sign that read, "Welcome Home, Gracie!"

And I burst into tears when I saw all they'd done.

Yes, I was truly home, and among friends.

Chapter Twenty-Three

A month has passed, and Jacques Station is a wonderland of snow and ice, bright twinkling lights, and lovely handmade Christmas wreaths. Children run about squealing with laughter as they fly around the sidewalks and down the small hills on their sleds, and adults and children are skating on the pond just outside the village.

Before the winter really set in, the people of Jacques Station got together to raise enough funds for a proper burial for old Harry Jakes to show there were no hard feelings even if he had almost burned the village to the ground.

Now the old man had a place in the village church cemetery and a small stone with his name and age engraved on it.

Even though Harry's careless actions with burning his trash had resulted in nearly burning the whole village down, there was room for forgiveness and remembrance. Some folks had objected to his cemetery burial and remembrance service at first, but kindness had prevailed.

After all, the old codger was a part of the history of Jacques Station, and we're a bunch of people who always want to remember—and learn from our past.

Soon after this ceremony, news came in that Sophia had been discovered hiding out in an abandoned barn some miles from the village. She was sick from cold and malnutrition, but the men who found her said she was no less vicious than the woman who had murdered four young drug dealers and tried to murder me.

That news was saddening, but Sophia was declared unfit to stand trial and was temporarily remanded to a facility for the mentally insane.

As Christmas approached, Allie told me she and Tina were thinking of getting married, and for Allie's sake, Tina and I made a tentative peace. I agreed to be Allie's bridesmaid and best man all rolled into one, and there was a quiet celebration at the manse.

Jack sent me photographs of himself with two beautiful, well-cared-for kittens, the two he'd adopted from Millie. I passed this on to Millie, who had tears of joy in her eyes to see her much-loved kittens in a good home.

We villagers decided to hold a big Christmas celebration party at the village hall, with decorations, and surprise gifts for the children.

The plan included a big Christmas feast, and everyone was invited, the money coming from a special account in the municipal council, supplemented by donations from the people who gave whatever they could.

Everyone attended, including the people who had moved away after losing their homes in the great fire. The McDonaghs and their two boys, who had stayed with us just after the fire and then found rented accommodation just outside the village, delighted us all by announcing that they had bought one of the big old houses in the village.

"It needs lots of work, but we can do it slowly," Sandy said, smiling at her husband.

"And we have two big strong boys to help with the

heavy work," her husband added, causing some eyerolls and groans from the two sons, whom I swear had each grown a good six inches taller since I'd last seen them.

Allie and I took a long walk before the festivities got going. Dressed in warm winter clothes, we were enchanted yet again to see the repaired homes and the progress that had gone into rebuilding the homes that had been so badly damaged they had to be demolished.

"It's wonderful that most of these new houses have been built in pretty much the same style as the original ones," Allie pointed out.

Elsie and Vera, who'd had a few sharp words from the police about their part in Sophia's murders of the drug dealers, were now happily sharing a small house in the village. They'd both been widowed several years ago, and they said that having company in sharing the home helped them to recover from their grief and loneliness. They both shared a sense of grief about the loss of their children to drugs, also, but they said the anger they had felt had dissipated with their very real sense of contentment in their new home.

"It looks like Jacques Station will live again," Allie declared, standing on the manse steps and looking out across the village towards the valley.

"We have a responsibility to see that happens," I said.

Despite all the activity, I had a few moments alone and felt again that sense of sorrow at being without my daughter, Becky. Maybe someday I would come to terms with the possibility that I would never know what happened to her. But in the meantime, I had a life to live.

Ben walked me home after the Christmas celebration, and we sat talking for hours, reminiscing about the past, and discussing our hopes for the future. One thing we did get sorted out was that the woman Anita, who had told me she and Ben were getting married, was actually his landlady. After he moved away from me, he'd rented a room in her house, along with several other people. It was, he said, a huge house. But he had come to realize that the woman was lonely and desperate for a relationship and had tried to develop one with just about every man who rented from her.

I actually felt sorry for her, eventually.

Because, at the end of the evening, Ben stayed over with me, and we rediscovered the feelings we had tried to push aside. If anything, there was a deeper sense that we belonged together.

I am not sure if our relationship will work, or if those divorce papers will be signed at some time later.

But one thing I know for sure, whatever the future holds, Jacques Station and its people will support each other and flourish, no matter what.

A word about the author...

Glenys O'Connell writes romantic suspense and comedy. Her interest in criminal psychology began when covering the crime beat as a journalist for a large daily newspaper . She holds a degree in psychology and is qualified as a counselor. As well as romance, she also writes non-fiction on mental health issues, children's books, and is an award-winning playwright. After years of travelling and working abroad, mainly in the UK & Ireland, she now makes her home in rural Ontario, Canada, with her husband, four grown-up children, and three spoiled cats. You can read more about her at her blog, https://romancecanbemurder.blogspot.com/ or on Facebook at www.facebook.com/glenys.oconnell www.glenysoconnell.com

Thank you for purchasing
this publication of The Wild Rose Press, Inc.

For questions or more information
contact us at
info@thewildrosepress.com.

The Wild Rose Press, Inc.
www.thewildrosepress.com

.